Praise for Nelson Aspen's

Kindred Spirits: A Titanic Tale

"Aspen's passion burns on every page, weaving history with wit and charm. A joy to read."

-Robert Jobson, New York Times bestselling author and royal expert

"Nelson Aspen swirls past and present with an original story that is neither for the faint of heart nor the closed of mind. Set a course for adventure and fasten your life belt."

-Steven Schwankert, "The Six"

"A beautifully crafted, sweet fantasy of timeless love. How refreshing for love and history to be served so nicely in a genuine page-turner."

-Jim Mackin, Historian & Author

"Kindred Spirits: A Titanic Tale" is charming, heartwarming, witty and sexy."

-Louise Shaffer, Author & Emmy Winning Actor

"One of the most unusual love stories you'll ever read with the bonus of being entertaining, informative and original."

-Carolyn Hennesy, Emmy Winning Actor & New York Times Bestselling Author.

"Nelson Aspen has outdone himself with *Kindred Spirits: A Titanic Tale*. He has crafted an engrossing reincarnation fantasy and expertly enhances his tale with interesting, historical details about the mighty ship and its passengers. Highly recommended."

-Tom Lisanti, author of "Ryan's Hope: An Oral History of Daytime's Groundbreaking Soap"

"A rollicking ride of a read where the heartbreaking conservatism of the 1910s meets the heart throbbing, homocrotic liberalism of the 2020s."

-Lloyd Burr, TV presenter and journalist

To the memory of Milton C. Long and all whose lives were lost or changed by the sinking of RMS Titanic.

"Sea of Life"
George Leo Robertson

Embarked on the sea of life,
Destiny and duration unknown,
Waters always changing,
Calm, peaceful, beautiful,
Fearful, dangerous, bleak,
All unpredictable, all uncontrolled.

But my ship is controlled.
For I guide it through the changing waters
With a mind and heart
Stronger and greater than the sea.

About the Author

Nelson Aspen is an award-winning journalist, author, and co-host of the popular "Titanic Talk" podcast. His previous novels include *Dancing Between the Raindrops* and *Dancing Between the Raindrops: The Hollywood Years* and a third installment in 2025 will complete the trilogy. His book *Your Home is Your Castle: Live Like an A-Lister in a Post Pandemic World* debuted at #1 on Amazon's Home Renovation and Remodel charts. He resides in New York City, and you may visit him at www.nelsonaspen.com or on social media @nelsonaspen.

FOREWORD

By: Paul Carganilla | Podcaster - "Titanic: Legacy" &
"COVEpod"

We have had over a century (112 years, to-the-moment I'm
writing this) to research and investigate the Titanic tragedy,
and yet, there are countless mysteries that continue to
surround Titanic's story today. Perhaps that is why our
interest and passion for Titanic continues to grow.

Her remains have been 12,500 feet beneath the surface since
1912, yet her boilers remain forever lit in our minds and
hearts. Is it the tragedy of over fifteen-hundred lives lost?
The cautionary tale of hubris in the Industrial Era? The
drama that plays out time-and-again through film, art, and
literature? The big mistakes or lapses in judgment? The
details of her design beauty?

In the mid-90's, James Cameron stood at the head-of-the-
table in a pitch meeting for 20th Century Fox executives. He
opened up Don Lynch & Ken Marschall's book *Titanic - An*

Illustrated History and said, "Imagine Romeo and Juliet...
on the Titanic."

For some Purists, creating fiction within the constructs of
the Titanic tragedy feels like blasphemy. Cameron knew his
fictional story would ruffle some feathers, but he also knew
he needed a tried-and-true formula to hook execs and fund
his movie. He was given the green light and went on to
create (what I consider to be) Hollywood's last "epic" film.
Cameron's 1997 *Titanic* told a new story, while keeping the
utmost reverence for Titanic's legacy. It was created with
love and respect, because James Cameron, himself, is a
Titanic Enthusiast.

Cameron's version would go on to re-invigorate her legacy
and introduce new generations to Titanic's story and the
impact it has had on Titanic's relevance is indisputable.
Instead of lying dormant on dusty bookshelves and black
and white movies, Titanic was re-launched onto the big
screen. This sparked generations of new fans and inspired
countless projects (some still in production today). The
creative fire that continues to burn is precisely what inspired

the launch of my own podcast, "Titanic: Legacy".

Cameron's film is only a single example. Consider the countless other movies, TV series, games and books that continue to keep Titanic in our hearts and minds and her value in fiction is abundantly clear.

It's imperative that these stories are told with appropriate love and respect for Titanic: by the enthusiasts who love and respect her most.

Much like the passengers on Titanic, today's 'Titanic Community 'is a fascinating mix of people and personalities from diverse backgrounds. Humans from a vast range of cultures, geographic regions, levels of education, and economic classifications still gather together to celebrate Titanic and her legacy. Today, however, instead of gathering on the ship, we gather on the "RMS World Wide Web". We share information, our collections, connections, experiences, interests, knowledge, hypotheses, and curiosities.

The first time I heard Nelson Aspen's voice, he was a guest on the podcast "Unsinkable: The Titanic Podcast". I sent

Nelson a "cold" message on Instagram, not expecting a response. One amazing thing I've learned about Titanic through social media: she continues to bring people together. Nelson graciously responded, and he has become a dear friend of my family.

Here's a man who has created his own legacy - telling peoples 'stories. For over three decades, Nelson Aspen has been a prolific entertainer and entertainment reporter. On stage, on the screen, and on the page, his unbridled creative energy continues to carry his work across the globe. From Los Angeles to New York City, the United Kingdom and Australia, Nelson has reported on the hottest topics in Hollywood and interviewed the brightest stars in show business.

As an author, he has published non-fiction works about style, celebrity, cuisine, and decor. Most-recently, he has been treating us to exquisitely-fun romps through the 80's, 90's, and "aughts", in a semi-autobiographical reflection on his life's journey, *Dancing Between the Raindrops*. *Kindred Spirits: A Titanic Tale* is Nelson's eighth book… and admittedly, this is the one I'm most personally excited about.

Nelson's connection to Titanic reaches across decades and dimensions. In the documentary *Ship of Dreams: Titanic Movie Diaries*, he recounts his life-long interest in the ship, his experiences on the Titanic Trail in Cobh, and his feeling of a past-life connection to Titanic victim Milton Clyde Long. Like most Titanic-fanatics, Nelson has been building his own collection over a lifetime and this book marks his first original addition.

I believe I know why our interest and passion for Titanic continues to grow:

*It's the ongoing research and non-fictional works and publications by scientists, explorers, historians and other experts.

*It's the endless creativity Titanic inspires - from television series and films (fiction and non-fiction), to artwork, stage performances, and books like the one you are reading now.

*It's the Community: following their hearts 'fire and keeping the memory of Titanic, her victims, survivors, and their families alive through conversation, research, factual publications, and inspired fiction.

*It's creators like Nelson Aspen who continue to spark our imagination as our thoughts swirl in the wake of the Ship of Dreams.

It's the people... and their stories.

Chapter One

April 14, 1912

Milton Clyde Long was adrift at sea.

Not literally, for the famed RMS Titanic ocean liner was steaming quickly from Southampton toward New York City on its maiden voyage, and Milton had been fortunate enough to secure a last minute First-Class Cabin D6 after a holiday tour in Europe. At 29, the only child of Springfield Massachusetts' esteemed Judge Charles Leonard Long and his wife Harriet was desperately trying to find some purpose in spite of all the privilege his family's wealth and position had always afforded him. He'd tried his hand at being a law clerk after stints at both Harvard and Columbia Universities, but felt as constrained by the profession and its demands as he did by the stiff collared black flannel suit men of his class were expected to wear when outside of their staterooms.

Described as a "gentleman of leisure," Milton searched aimlessly for something to ignite a passion inside him. He couldn't find it in the Paris bistros or concert halls. Winter revelries in Switzerland failed to stimulate him. He assumed it unlikely to be waiting for him in New York at the

Metropolitan Opera House or Museum of Natural History.
His parents doted on him and indulged any whim he
expressed, but Milton's serious, somber side kept him from
ever having any truly excitable moments like other young
men his age, most of whom were already married or
seriously courting well-bred young society ladies. He
despised small talk and the social rituals that went along
with navigating polite Edwardian society.

Milton had met comely Gretchen Fiske Longley, 22,
on the first day of the voyage when a steward had shown
him to his cabin. Gretchen and her two maternal aunts were
occupying the adjacent staterooms with a maid, and it was
apparent from their fawning and flirtatious manners that
they saw Milton as eligible prey for the recent graduate of
the Boston Ladies School. Her aunt Cornelia Andrews, of
course, knew of the Longs by reputation and found it a lucky
coincidence that they would be sailing back to the United
States together.

While he may not have had the charisma of a
Casanova or any professional cachet attached to him, Milton
was a catch, nonetheless. Most importantly, he was a
wealthy young man from a respected family and, even at his
shyest and quietest, was also considered somewhat
attractive. He stood 5'10 and had a fair complexion with

dark brown hair and unique gray-blue eyes. His face was thin and angular but conveyed masculine strength with his strong, curved nose and square forehead. He had full lips, which he instinctively kept pursed when closed, a carryover from his mother's reprimands when he was a child, not to breathe through his mouth and let it hang open "lest all the flies come in." It consequently made him look as though he was perpetually smirking, but given his position in society that was hardly an unusual demeanor.

The four days of the voyage thus far had passed by uneventfully, with Milton spending most of his time writing letters, strolling the decks, and alternately reading the two books he had brought along, both of which were current best sellers: J.M. Barrie's *Peter Pan* and Edith Wharton's *Ethan Frome*. He was compelled by both, precisely because of how differently each seemed to tap into his own feelings of futility and unfocus.

Peter Pan was much more mischievous and adventuresome than Milton could ever fathom being, but the metaphor of never being able to grow up and escape childhood resonated with him. Massachusetts protagonist, Ethan Frome, struggled with the despair and forbidden sexual undercurrents of being attracted to his wife's vivacious cousin. This, too, was something Milton understood—desires that not only had to be masked but squelched.

For the only thing that ever seemed to set Milton's heart fluttering was the beauty of male pulchritude and the qualities displayed by those who possessed it. He felt the arousal and desire when he stood before the statue of Michaelangelo's *David* or Horatio Greenough's neoclassical depiction of George Washington. He lingered too long at the nude works by DaVinci and Moser, wondering if anyone noticed his unusual fascination that went beyond the brushstrokes. On the rare occasion that Milton encountered such specimens in the real world, rowing in the Charles River or tossing a ball outside Harvard Hall, he instinctively avoided even so much as eye contact. In his world, even the smallest such impropriety could leave one's reputation permanently tarnished or even ruined.

He admired a prominent, high-profile older couple of first-class gentlemen passengers, former aide to President Theodore Roosevelt, Archibald Butt, and classical artist, Francis David Millet. They had been on a European holiday when they boarded Titanic and hobnobbed with the likes of celebrities such as the Duff-Gordons, the Astors, and Benjamin Guggenheim. The men had built a large mansion together in Washington DC and were known to host lavish parties there for the political elite. They had shared a stateroom on their previous sailing from Berlin, and the subsequent whispers had propelled them to book separate rooms on Titanic, even though they were only ever seen in each other's company. It was titillating for Milton to imagine sharing such close quarters with another man. Even in school dormitories and on holiday outings, he never had to bunk in with anyone else. Would Butt and Millet maintain a degree of modesty in their private confines, or be unabashedly open?

Also traveling as a couple were two handsome American tennis stars, Richard Norris Williams and Karl Behr, although there was no hint of scandal there; it was not uncommon even for first-class male passengers to share accommodations and these two athletes in particular seemed to welcome every opportunity to display their masculine virility in the ship's gymnasium and with various attentive, admiring females. This pair, Milton surmised, would surely have felt no inhibitions between them. In fact, he likened their impressive physiques to the famous *The Swimming Hole* painting of six male nude bathers by Thomas Eakins, with its intoxicating depiction of smooth, sculpted torsos, biceps and buttocks.

There was no shortage of notable figures among Titanic's passenger list, not limited to but including the world's richest man John Jacob Astor and wife Madeleine. There was "nouveau riche" mining magnate Margaret ""Brown, the owner of Macy's department store Isidor Straus, and famed movie personality Dorothy Gibson. It was an all-around gay voyage for first-class travelers, but even so, Milton mostly opted to keep his nose in his books when he wasn't partaking in meals with his refined and reserved tablemates. He would occasionally smoke a cigarette and had a habit of pocketing match books when he'd find them lying about.

It was the evening of April 14, however, when he could no longer look away.

A young man Milton had noticed periodically from the time he had embarked from Cherbourg was now directly in his line of vision at the dining table where he was listening to Gretchen's Aunt Anna espouse her viewpoints on the recent Triangle Shirtwaist Factory fire in New York City. Doors to stairwells and exits had been locked and 146 garment workers, mostly young immigrant women, had been burned to death or killed when leaping from upper story windows. It was a disastrous scenario too horrific to imagine, but impossible to escape from conversations about current events.

"I'm simply terrified by fire," he heard Anna saying as he poked around at his salmon hollandaise and tried to catch a glimpse of the young man sitting a few tables away. "I'll gladly take my chances at sea."

"As if anything could happen on a ship as mighty as this one," her sister replied. "Everyone agrees it is unsinkable."

Milton himself was unconcerned about maritime safety. Not only was the White Star Line's reputation for safety second to none, he had already experienced a shipwreck the year before while traveling on an Alaskan tourist excursion aboard the SS Spokane. The ship's hull was torn open by a rock but was able to navigate to shallow waters where it was towed to shore. There had only been one fatality, and most people considered sea travel, especially on a ship like Titanic, worry-free. Besides, he loved being on the water, whether it was the wide open North Atlantic, a leisurely excursion along the Seine in a bateau mouche, or rowing in Crystal Lake back home. Ironically, he had never particularly cared for or excelled at swimming.

The young man Milton had been watching was tall and thin, with thick light brown hair and a flawless complexion the color of cream. Impeccably dressed in a perfectly tailored navy blue three-piece suit that clung to his trim physique, he appeared to be in his late teens or early twenties. Most notable to Milton, however, who was sporting his own custom-made, monogrammed ensemble, was his exuberant personality. He spoke animatedly almost with his entire body and not just his mouth; gesturing with his hands and widening his large, expressive eyes. He sat in between two older individuals who appeared to be his parents and was openly affectionate with them both. Their adoration for him appeared in their faces and they alternately laughed at his repartee and beamed with pride. They had their elbows on the table, casually, which would ordinarily have been a breach of dining etiquette, but the entire party was strikingly elegant in their merriment. Even with the buzz of conversation, tinkling glassware and sterling silverware clicking against china, Milton could hear that laughter. It was as intoxicating as the wine he had been sipping to avoid having to join the conversation about the factory fire.

Frances Millet walked over from his own table to join the family of three and extend greetings. They were

obviously socially connected, and the elegantly dressed
matriarch welcomed him warmly. She even extended her
hand which he delicately held as he bestowed a kiss upon it.
Milton studied her good-looking son, watching him interact
with an ease and conviviality that belied his youth. Milton
wondered what it would be like to kiss his hand.

He tuned out the chatter coming from Gretchen and
her aunts, somehow managing to focus his hearing on the
more distant conversation where the youthful beauty was
seated. Millet was suggesting they retire to the A la Carte
restaurant to enjoy after dinner coffees, an offer that was
enthusiastically accepted, and they began to exchange good-
night pleasantries to the other passengers at their table.

Milton would ordinarily have looked away, but he
was too besotted and needed to see what would happen next,
keeping his gaze focused on the lean young man who held
the chair for his mother as she rose from her place. To
Milton's utter surprise, it was at that precise moment that
they locked eyes for the first time. Milton felt himself gasp
for air as his heart began to pound in his chest.

Their little coterie seemed to glide past his table, but
the magnificent tall one was bringing up the rear, seeming to
tarry so that he could maintain his almost brazen stare at
Milton. Milton realized he was holding his breath but

couldn't manage to exhale as long as their eyes were fixed on each other. The beauty's thick hair was immaculately cut and parted on the side, lightly oiled to make it shine vibrantly. Milton noticed how his small ears protruded from the sides of his head, and his broad shoulders sloped a bit.

Unabashed, as he approached Milton, he extended his hand in greeting and broke into a wide, friendly smile. Almost in a daze, Milton managed to raise his arm and accept an awkward handshake.

"Don't get up, mate. Just wanted to say, Good Evening."

Thunderstruck, Milton swallowed hard and realized he was half standing, half sitting in his instinct to preserve some semblance of protocol. Every time he'd caught sight of this fellow, it was obvious how gregarious and charming he was to anyone and everyone. And rather than be envious, Milton was as ardently captivated as others around him.

Accustomed to guiding polite conversation, the young man continued, "Jack Thayer. We haven't met yet. But I've seen you on deck and in the Salon."

He finally managed to say, flattered, "Milton Long. Of Springfield, Massachusetts."

"A great American city I've never had the pleasure to visit. Yet."

Jack's parents had paused with Millet and turned to face him.

"Mother and Father, this is Mr. Long of Massachusetts. My parents, John and Marian of Philadelphia."

Milton was now on his feet and bowed his head, respectfully. "An honor to make your acquaintances, Mr. and Mrs. Thayer."

In total command of the social situation, Jack encouraged his parents to go enjoy their coffees with Mr. Millet but, "I think I'll take a few turns around the deck to help digest that large dinner. Perhaps I can persuade Mr. Long to join me."

Meekly, Milton nodded in the affirmative. He placed his napkin down and nervously said, "Good evening, ladies," to Gretchen and her aunts. He'd somehow started breathing again, even if he wasn't sure when it had resumed. His stomach was churning with trepidation at being one-on-one with this magnificent-looking person who had just invited him for a stroll. Few of his peers had ever been so forthright in seeking out his companionship, and it resulted in a newfound exhilaration.

The pair moved out of the dining room to climb the Grand Staircase that would lead them to the First-Class

Promenade on A-Deck. Jack kept the conversation going as they proceeded.

"We've been on holiday in Europe. Germany, mostly. But my siblings stayed home. We'll all be having a fiftieth birthday celebration for my father when we get back. They're planning everything. We boarded at Cherbourg, but I think you were already aboard by then, no?"

Milton gave no indication that he had already taken notice of Jack's point of embarkation.

"Yes. I came on in Southampton."

"I wish I could stay and enjoy Manhattan when we get there, but it will be straight onto the train back to Philadelphia. Springtime is really lovely there. I suspect it arrives a bit later in Massachusetts?"

Milton was thinking what a valiant job he was doing with polite banter, but it took all Milton's self-control not to stare dumbstruck at Jack's handsome, smiling face. Jack explained that he was a freshman at Yale and planned to eventually follow his father into the railroad business.

As Jack spoke, Milton's eyes remained fixed on his sparkling eyes and a perfect mouth that was uniquely expressive as he painted pictures with every word and inflection. He had an adjective to describe everything. School was "ripping" and "jolly," even if the faculty were "archaic" or "droll." Milton had never seen anyone so animated without being flamboyant. The energy and enthusiasm Jack exuded wasn't just attractive. It was infectious.

When they finally made their way to the sliding doors to access the Promenade deck, Jack asked, "Will you be warm enough in that suit? At least I have a vest underneath." He opened the lapels of his suit coat to show off the vest and Milton took a deep breath to steady himself. The interaction may not have been outwardly intimate, but it was a first of its kind experience for Milton.

"I'll be fine. I never get cold."

Jack patted him on the arm, jovially. "Must be that hearty New England stock, eh?"

They stepped outside onto the deck, and both winced at the blast of cold air they instantly felt.

"Wowza!" Jack exclaimed. "It's really dropped since before dinner. Stick close to me, Sport."

Milton felt the cold, but it didn't penetrate him. He was too gobsmacked. They began to stroll at a brisk pace in a futile effort to stay warm. Jack's gift of gab was relentless, and he was most certainly a "gigglemug," what the older generation would refer to as someone wearing a constant smile.

"Have you been on holiday?" Jack asked his new friend.

"I was skiing in St. Moritz. I wanted to go on the Cresta. The season is only a few months, but my parents talked me out of it. Too risky."

"I think your parents have a point. Racing a toboggan down an ice track sounds terrifying. I'll stick with cricket, thanks."

Milton's chest puffed out a bit. "I don't scare easily."

"Ice skating suits me for winter sport. Your parents were with you?"

Milton shook his head. "Let's say they can be very persuasive even from across the ocean. Perhaps they'll finally be less overprotective when I turn thirty this year."

Jack laughed and told him, "Mate, I'd've put you at twenty-one."

Milton felt himself flush, even in the frigid cold and confessed, "The crowd is young in Switzerland, so I masqueraded as twenty-two."

"I'm sure they believed it, "Jack said, leading them to the railing. Together, they looked up at the night sky.

"Brilliant stars. I wish I'd paid more attention in astronomy class. But where's the moon?"

Suddenly finding his words, Milton smirked.
"Maybe it's too cold to come out."

Jack laughed again, genuinely amused. "It's the kind
of night that makes one feel glad to be alive."

Milton was mystified and impressed by his new
friend's indomitable optimism even as he added, "I heard
there were reports of ice fields, but I haven't seen any, have
you? It hasn't seemed to slow us down much."

Jack shook his head and spoke knowledgeably
enough to pass for a sailor himself. "When the sea is this
calm, you'd think bergs would be easy to spot, but if there's
no water to break at their bases, it's just the opposite."

"Well, if the Captain decides to slow down, that's
fine with me. I'm not in a hurry to get back."

Jack finally ceased the small talk and looked at his
new friend with apparent concern.

"Something unpleasant waiting for you?"

"No," Milton confessed with some melancholy.
"Nothing is waiting for me at all."

"Mate, I don't buy that for a second. You're sailing
First-Class on the maiden voyage of the world's greatest-
ever feat of engineering on your way home from a European
adventure."

"It's been more reading than rollicking, actually. I wish I had your joie-de-vivre, Jack."

Jack used his shoulder to give Milton a nudge that seemed more sweet than chummy and softly told him, "We'll have to work on that, Chuckaboo."

For him to have used the affectionate slang to describe a good friend resulted in a moment of silence that felt private and personal for both of them.

They made their way around to the starboard side of the Boat Deck and meandered past the brightly lit gymnasium, considered a highly innovative amenity with its state-of-the-art exercise devices like an electric horse, mechanical bicycles, and weightlifting machines. Through the beautiful arched windows, they noticed the specially engaged "Physical Educator," a short but sturdy Scotsman named Thomas W. McCawley. He was dressed in his white flannel uniform and going about his nightly closing rituals of wiping down the machines and extinguishing the lights.

Even though the facility was open to first-class passengers for the cost of a mere shilling per person, Milton had avoided paying a visit, having immediately perceived a judgmental scowl from McCawley. He had narrow eyes that seemed to squint disapprovingly at Milton's mild-mannered demeanor, or so Milton perceived. The tennis stars Williams and Behr certainly hadn't faced such snobbery, as Milton had witnessed their frivolity all around the ship. He was envious that their fitness and celebrity afforded them a free pass to immediate acceptance wherever they went. No wonder they were so comfortable in their own skins, a confidence Milton couldn't imagine for himself.

"I went a few rounds on the punching bag yesterday," Jack commented with cheer. "Old Man Thomas wasn't too impressed, but I told him all my strength and power are in my legs."

Milton hoped they would pass unnoticed by the steely looking health expert who had a unique and annoying knack of conveying disdain on anyone he saw as weak, even members of a higher social caste than his own.

"Well, I haven't been too impressed with Old Man Thomas," Milton admitted.

"Hah! Touche!"

They finished their first turn around the deck. Jack was shivering when he said, "At least during the day you can get some hot soup or tea out here."

Milton looked up into Jack's azure eyes that made him seem older and wiser than either of them. Neither could express the mood of the moment, so Jack came to the rescue by suggesting they "go have that coffee" and Milton said, "That sounds perfect."

By the time they arrived at the A la Carte restaurant, the elder Thayers had departed, presumably to retire for the evening as it was already after ten, as indicated on the *Honour and Glory Crowning Time* clock that adorned the first landing of the Grand Staircase. It was one of the ship's most extravagant and popular art pieces.

The expansive room was exquisitely designed in the luxurious Louis XVI Versailles style with walnut paneling and gilt-brass accents, an honorific imitation of the swanky Ritz-Carlton Hotel. Even the most seasoned and savvy travelers were impressed by the chic elegance of its decor. The only other gentleman nearby was the middle-aged Adolphe Saalfeld, a German-born chemist who now lived in England and was en route to New York to market his line of concentrated perfumes and fragrances. Jack recognized him from having passed each other frequently on C-Deck, where he also occupied a First-Class cabin. They nodded to each other in a cordial greeting as an Italian waiter walked them to a small table underneath a large oval mirror. It was a secluded location and Milton preferred to muse that the waiter had intuited that they were craving privacy.

Jack ordered them two coffees and remarked how much the lovely room resembled the Ritz from which it had been inspired.

"If I didn't know better, I'd swear I was in Paris!"

By the time their beverages arrived, the men's polite conversation was winding down, and they sipped in silence until Jack eventually took out his pocket watch to check the time. Milton wished he could come up with something else to say because the one thing he didn't want to utter was "Good night."

"Mother has been fighting off the ardent attention of Mr. Ismay, so I'm saving her by being her Bridge partner in the morning," Jack finally said, almost wistfully. "So, I'd better get myself back to my stateroom. I wish we had met sooner."

Milton brightened, wishing it, too.

"Well, better late than never."

"That's the spirit, I say," Jack grinned.

Milton folded his napkin. "Thank you for the camaraderie, Jack."

"The pleasure was indeed mine. I'm sure I'll see you around tomorrow. Maybe if it warms up a bit we can take another turn around the deck, and you can tell me more about St. Moritz. If you were fudging your age, I suspect there must be more of a story there and I want to hear it."

"I'd like that," he said, casting his eyes down to his lap while Jack rose from the table.

"And Milton, incidentally…"

Milton lifted his gaze and looked up at the winsome Jack Thayer.

"You're always welcome to come for a visit in Philadelphia. Our family loves hosting houseguests."

Milton couldn't ever remember his parents welcoming overnight guests into their Springfield home. It was amazing how two families from the same social world could be so different.

No more words were exchanged between them, and Jack headed out of the restaurant to walk back to his cabin on C-Deck. The waiter watched him exit and then cast a glance over at Milton, who noticed and worried that it was a look of disapproval.

When Milton finally ambled back to his own stateroom it was after eleven. After carefully hanging his suit jacket in the closet and loosening his tie and stiff shirt collar, he sat in the armchair across from the bed and picked up *Ethan Frome*, intending to read for a while until he felt sleepy. But staring at the page, none of the words were in focus. All he could see were Jack's sparkling blue eyes and those full lips stretched into a wide smile. He'd even been charmed by the way his Adam's apple moved up and down his neck. Milton was fully smitten.

It was a dangerous, unacceptable feeling that made him tremble with a mixture of fear and pleasure. Even if he had to hide it, he was determined to embrace it.

He nodded off, the book in his lap, while remembering the strength of Jack's handshake when they first touched, hours before.

The reverie was short-lived, when he was woken by an urgent knock at the door. His mind still cloudy, his first thought, was it Jack?

Milton opened the door to William, the efficient steward who attended the cabins on D-deck. Without hesitation, William crossed the threshold into the room and to the closet. It was not quite midnight.

"Pardon the interruption, sir," William said, moving quickly. "The Captain has asked all passengers to come on deck at once. Please dress warmly."

Suddenly the omnipresent hum of Titanic's engines stopped, and the men shared a moment of surprised eye contact in reaction to the sudden silence.

William turned back to the closet and pulled out the white life jacket that was stored on the top shelf. He spoke matter-of-factly with his clipped Yorkshire accent. "And please wear your life vest, Mister Long. May I assist you in putting it on?"

Remembering his experience aboard the S.S. Spokane, he answered, "No, that's all right, I know how to do it. What's happened?"

"Likely we've thrown a propeller blade. Wouldn't surprise me on a maiden voyage. It happened on her sister ship, Olympic, just two months ago. Shouldn't cause too much of a delay."

William walked out of the room without looking at Milton again, simply adding, "See you on deck, sir."

Now clad in his full suit, heavy tweed topcoat, and life vest, Milton could hear the start of some commotion in the corridor as William exited. He planned to look for Jack on deck, welcoming the unexpected opportunity to see him again so soon.

Finding all the layers he was wearing to be cumbersome, Milton took his time making his way to the deck. He was imagining the friendship he and Jack would continue to cultivate for the remainder of the voyage. Was it terrible to hope that the thrown propellor blade would delay the journey a day or more? Perhaps that would be ample time to convince Jack to visit him in Springfield, or maybe he would take the Thayers up on the offer to come to Philadelphia. His mind raced with the possibilities he could plan.

Arriving on deck, he saw perhaps two dozen First-Class passengers still gathered inside, hesitant to go out into the frigid night air. One of Titanic's pianists, Theodore Brailey, could be heard playing a merry tune, and there was a feeling of lightheartedness, even whimsy, as if everyone was participating in some sort of game. Many were laughing at the absurdity of wearing the bulky canvas and cork life jackets over their finery or nightclothes, especially on an unsinkable ship.

Milton did not see the Thayers among them, so he continued to mill about until an officer approached him and asked, "Might we ask you to step out on deck, sir? We are trying to encourage the women and children to enter into the lifeboats and we could use some assistance from the gentlemen."

"Lifeboats?" Milton repeated. "I thought we had just thrown a propeller blade."

"No, sir," the Officer said politely. "We struck an iceberg. Probably nothing our watertight compartments can't handle, but for safety's sake the Captain has ordered women and children to wait it out in the lifeboats."

"Certainly," he replied, numbly. It couldn't have been significant if he had slept right through it, and he trusted the officer's nonchalance. To the naked eye, there seemed nothing amiss with the vessel, especially with music playing and all the lights burning brightly. Perhaps he could detect a slight list to the port side, but that wouldn't be unexpected when at sea, he knew from past experience.

He looked at his gold watch that read twelve fifteen in the morning. Bracing for the temperature, he plunged his hands into his coat pockets, lamenting that he had left his gloves back in the cabin. He followed some others coerced by the officer to proceed outside. There, scores of passengers were huddled around as crew members worked to persuade and assist women and children to enter the lifeboats. He noticed well-known film actress, Dorothy Gibson, and her mother among them. She seemed every inch the star as she pushed past them, still trying to make sense of all the commotion.

"If you want to put us in the lifeboats, why not be quick about it and not leave us to stand out here freezing? Is that what First-Class passage gets us on the White Star Line?"

They couldn't be blamed for their hesitation to leave the comfort and perceived safety of Titanic to climb into a wooden boat and be lowered shakily down into the icy, dark sea below. He recognized John Jacob Astor, who was helping Madeleine and her maid settle into the tilting Lifeboat number 4. There was a rumor that she was pregnant, and it was confirmed when he heard the multimillionaire asking Second Officer Lightoller if he could accompany his wife since she was "in a delicate condition." The request was denied.

Some of the string musicians had now arrived on deck and were playing upbeat music which only made the atmosphere more surreal. A white rocket was fired and exploded high in the air above them, resembling fireworks. The civility of the scene was short-lived when ear-splitting roars of steam began to scream from the funnels, a result of the ship's engines shutting down.

Milton could now clearly see that Titanic's bow had dipped beneath the ocean's surface, and he fully appreciated the gravity of the moment. His teeth chattering, he decided to step back inside for just a moment to warm himself and had to maneuver around the crush of dozens more passengers pushing to get out on deck.

That is when he saw Jack, his blue eyes wide with alarm. Milton called out his name, and a momentary look of relief came over Jack.

"Milton, have you seen my parents? We went back to our cabins to get topcoats but then became separated."

"I haven't. They must be somewhere out on deck. Or maybe already in a lifeboat."

"I hope so. Although I don't think they're letting any men board, unless they're crew. Some of them aren't even full."

"Let's head to the stern. Perhaps we'll find them there."

The further back on the ship, the safer they would be, Milton reasoned.

Jack's anxiety emboldened Milton to become protective. "I wouldn't worry, Jack. When I was aboard the stricken Spokane, we were towed by a rescue ship. Everybody made it off safely. Well, except for one poor chap."

Inside the nearby gymnasium, now ablaze with light and packed with passengers seeking momentary respite from the frigid night air, Milton noticed Thomas McCawley, ruddy cheeked and still in his white flannels. Although not wearing a life vest himself, the sportsman was assisting others into theirs. Milton observed a little girl, aged about ten, amusing herself on the rowing machine and oblivious to the frenzied scene played out around her. She may be needing that skill soon enough, he thought with dark irony.

By the time they made it to the stern, the situation had become more chaotic, and people were scrambling around the deck, calling out to one another and trying to be heard over the horrible sounds coming from the funnels. Some women were crying and screaming, and passengers from second- and third-class had now arrived on deck and were clamoring for admission into the lifeboats. From the other side of the ship, they heard gunshots ring out in a futile attempt to restore orderly conduct. Even more frightening for Jack, there was no sign of his mother or father.

They watched as boat number 8 was being launched. The lovely Countess of Rothes was among the mere twenty-eight people aboard. The likable elderly couple, Ida and Isidor Straus, had been offered seats but they could see Isidor refusing to disobey the "women and children first" protocol, and his wife would not leave his side.

"There's plenty of room still left," Jack remarked. "It can't hurt to ask."

Milton put his hand against one of the large lifeboat davits with its cantilevered arm. Jack asked the crewman if they could use two able-bodied young men to help row.

There was no persuading them. There would be no room for male passengers aboard any of the boats and the crewman brusquely pushed Milton's hand off of the davit to begin the business of loading and lowering. Chief Purser McElroy advised them, "Stay on the ship as long as you can then make a swim for it until you can be picked up in the water. Your vests will keep you afloat but be quick about it. The water is damned cold. You won't last long."

Water could be seen moving more quickly up from the ship's bow, and they instinctively hurried away from it, the stern rising ever higher out of the sea. Things inside the ship were coming apart and sliding around, adding to the strange cacophony all around them.

"Blazes! I hadn't counted on going swimming tonight, that's for sure," Jack said with a feeble attempt at levity.

"You're sporty, aren't you?"

"I don't think my cricket skills will be of much use tonight. How about you?"

"Not so much, I'm afraid. I never got to try the Cresta, remember?" Milton's habitual smirk inadvertently added to the gallows humor.

Jack put his arm around Milton's shoulder in a fraternal gesture and cajoled, "Tonight you're going to be a regular Jim Thorpe."

Even over his heavy coat and life vest, the feeling of Jack's arm was comforting to Milton, and he allowed himself to feel it as an affectionate moment.

They went to the railing and looked down at the horrific scene playing out around and below them. Crew members were struggling to lower the lifeboats from their davits, people were starting to jump and fall into the water, more white rockets were being fired and frightened, dazed crowds were scurrying in all directions. Milton could have sworn he spotted White Star's Managing Director Bruce Ismay in one of the boats. Obviously, even in First-Class, some tiers of privilege were higher than others. Especially under such dire circumstances.

The lights burning from inside the ship began to flicker, and a woeful groan began from inside her bowels.

Jack pointed to a small cluster of lifeboats rowing away from the stricken ship.

"We should head for those while we can. They'll pick us up."

Milton nodded. "Sounds like a good plan."

"Shall we climb down the ropes? It looks to be about sixty feet."

Quickly evaluating the ropes, Milton knew he lacked the upper body strength to shimmy down, but he observed the railing and patted it. "I can't manage that, but I think I can ride this down to the water."

"Like sliding on a banister. Brilliant!"

Their adrenaline was pumping, and Milton was surprised to find himself smiling as he hoisted himself up to straddle the slanting starboard rail, near the second funnel which was tilting precariously. If Jack believed in him, it gave him the confidence to believe in himself, for once.

"You coming, boy?" he asked the beautiful Jack Thayer.

"I'm going to jump out as far as I can. Be sure to push yourself away from the ship as soon as you reach the water. You have to avoid suction or getting tangled up. Make a swim for it and I'll be with you in a minute. You still owe me the story about St. Moritz."

Milton took one more moment to look into his face before adding, "I'll see you in New York."

If he could have gone back on deck and grabbed Jack, he would have. They could cling together while the water washed over them. Death together would be better than being separated this way.

"I can't wait."

Milton descended along the side of the ship, watching the surface of the water get closer and closer, now only ten feet below. It was black and churning as Titanic slid deeper.

But there was no swimming possible for Milton Long. Before he could release his grip from the railing, he was pulled down. In an instant, he was underwater and one of the first of more than 1500 of Titanic's casualties.

Chapter Two

One moment, he was looking down at the inky waters moving ever more swiftly close, and he instinctively closed his eyes tightly and held his breath as he was sucked into it, the bitter cold slicing him like knives and then filling his lungs. But a second later when he managed to open his eyes, he was suddenly free from the freezing pain, nor did he see any debris or even the massive hulk of Titanic looming over him.

He saw the olive-skinned face of another man, attractive and brown-eyed, right up against his own, and as he gasped to inhale, he realized their lips had been pressed together. It startled him every bit as much as the sight of the ship's stern rising high out of the Atlantic.

He wasn't in the water, although he was soaking wet. With perspiration. He was standing in the middle of a crowd but there were no Astors, Thayers, Guggenheims, or Strauses among them. They were all men, many scantily clad and dancing wildly underneath multicolored flickering lights. The thunderous roar of the massive boilers ripping through the structure of the ship had been replaced with a booming, pulsating kind of wild music he could never remember hearing before.

"It's Milton, isn't it?" the swarthy man asked, provocatively running a hand up and down his arm. There was a tattoo of an eagle's head on his neck, peering up from under his shirt collar.

"No, it's Preston," he corrected. "But it's impossible to hear in here. Let's go to the bar."

This wasn't the first time Preston had mistakenly been called "Milton." It had happened a few times over the years with delivery people or customer service reps on the telephone. It always struck him as odd because he enunciated well (he was an actor, after all) and the two names really weren't that similar. Besides, who the hell was named "Milton" in 2024!?

Preston and Eagle Neck arrived at the bar at the other end of the room, across from the dance floor. The line was jammed with thirsty guys pushing and clamoring to get the attention of the half-naked, oiled up bartenders. It was worse than the crush of dudes queuing up for the bathrooms and Preston, even though he was only twenty-nine, felt exhausted.

He'd flirted and danced and had a few cocktails. He'd turned down offers of coke and ecstasy. Nameless dude was attractive, but Preston didn't have it in him to continue the ritual required to lure him back uptown to his apartment for a hookup that had no guarantees of quality or duration, so he shouted over the pounding music to try and politely duck out.

"I'm going to call it a night and head home. I'll catch you later, man."

The guy didn't look too disappointed, so it let Preston off the hook from feeling guilty and he navigated his way through the crowds of men in various stages of inebriation, toward the exit.

He muttered to himself, "Why the fuck do I even bother?"

His phone sounded the familiar notification from the Grindr app he'd left open, but he ignored it, too fed up and spent to pursue a random quickie.

Once outside on Ninth Avenue, he took a great gulp of the cool April air. He was grateful to be out of the noisy club and into the comparatively serene atmosphere of a Manhattan night, where the only sounds were honking horns from taxis, some sirens, and the occasional passing music from someone's car or a Pedi-Cab. It was such a pleasant evening, and still relatively early at only eleven, he decided to forgo calling an Uber and catch the subway at Columbus Circle.

He had just missed the 1 local train, so it was nearly twenty minutes before the next one arrived. He restlessly moved about the platform, the southern end of which always had a strange stench of something mingled between spoiled milk and urine. He was trying to dodge an aggressive panhandler, a candy-selling migrant mother with a baby strapped to her back, and an enormous, curious rat scrounging around for some morsels to eat. Preston regretted that he hadn't just kept walking northward up to his apartment on 84th and Riverside. It would have been faster.

He second-guessed himself about having left the club. If he'd done a bump of cocaine, he reasoned, he'd have gotten his second wind and would probably still be there dancing and flirting. Maybe even a little anonymous action in a bathroom stall.

By the time a train arrived and he started rolling his way underground to the 86th Street station, Preston wondered if he was slowing down because of his age. Here he was heading home before midnight. And hangovers weren't as easy to brush off as they used to be. Is this what it was going to be like going forward now that he could see "the Big 3-0" on the horizon? He decided he would have to take an extra tough Peloton cycling class the next day to prove otherwise to himself.

Once home to his cozy one-bedroom apartment on tree-lined 84th Street, the block renamed in honor of one-time resident Edgar Allen Poe, Preston brushed his teeth before stripping off his club clothes and flopping into bed. He took only a moment to switch on the white-noise machine atop his chest of drawers before drifting off to sleep.

But Milton was still awake, even though he hadn't seen or heard anything since he'd felt the lips of that man in the noisy place with the flashing light. Was he still under water? Was it some kind of hallucination? Everything seemed peaceful for the moment, and his breathing was deep, calm, and steady like the gentle rolling of the sea he remembered when walking the deck with Jack before the iceberg struck the ship. Maybe this is what the afterlife was.

The horrid, raucous sounds were no longer part of his consciousness. Instead, he recollected an Anglican hymn. "Eternal Father, strong to save, whose arm hath bound the restless wave, who bids the mighty ocean deep, its own appointed limits keep. Oh, hear us when we cry to Thee, for those in peril on the sea."

Milton tried to utter the words, but he possessed no power of speech. He felt like a soul without form, yet the lyrics seemed to swirl around him. After the terror of plummeting from the doomed Titanic, this condition wasn't worrisome, merely confounding. He would wait and see what unfolded next.

He would only have to wait a few more hours.

※ ※ ※

Preston woke feeling unusually refreshed and clear headed. It had really helped that he'd only had a couple cocktails and abstained from any recreational drugs the night before, and he'd enjoyed a rare, undisturbed night's sleep free from dreams or a trip to the bathroom. It was shortly after eight, and he double-checked his phone to make certain he didn't have any auditions to worry about. The only thing on his schedule was a voice lesson in the afternoon, so he could take his time and go for a workout. Outside the window, he could see that it was a sunny, early Spring morning so he decided he would opt for the latter.

After making himself a cup of coffee with his handy Keurig machine, he sat on one of the two stools at his kitchen's mini bar and sipped, contentedly. Ordinarily, he would have woken up with a little hangover and probably beside some cute twink or Zaddy he'd lured home at "last call." This solitude was somehow discomforting. He regretted not answering the Grindr message.

He'd be turning thirty in the fall and his best friend, Greg, was already pressing him to start making extravagant plans to celebrate. He'd been hesitant about it, not because he was freaked out by the milestone number, but because he was starting to feel less and less inclined to go wild at any and every opportunity. Was this developing maturity age-related, he wondered.

Preston valued his independence. While most of his peer group had already paired off or were constantly in the pursuit of finding "the one," he ascribed to being alone but not lonely. No boyfriend, no pets, not even any plants to care for. He was free to accept any acting job, modeling gig or jet-setting fling that came along at any time. He could just close the door to his apartment and go wherever he wanted for as long as he wanted.

It seemed like an enviable position, even if it struck his parents as a bit worrisome.

"When are you to get over this show business thing and find a real job?" his father had been asking at every holiday meal for years.

Whenever they pressed too hard, he would call them by their first names, Brandon and Liz, rather than "Dad and

Mom." It was a not-so-subtle signal that it was an off-limits topic and, most of the time, they would back off. As an only child, Preston knew he had a special place in their hearts that allowed him more leeway than others. He had always used it to his advantage, from having his curfews extended to increased allowances.

"Honey, don't you want to settle down and find yourself one special person?" his mother usually inquired in their regular phone calls.

After a second cup of coffee, Preston donned his favorite loose fitting Under Armor running shorts that showed off his buttocks and paired it with a comfortable old race singlet from a half-marathon he'd run a few years earlier with the New York Road Runners. He had spent a year as a member of the city's most popular LGBTQ+ running club, FrontRunners, until he'd slept his way through all the sexiest teammates. He grabbed his favorite Yankees cap to pull over his wavy brown hair, still sticking out in "bed-head" style. For some reason, he didn't feel like listening to music on his run this morning, so he left the ear buds behind after lacing up his favorite pair of Saucony sneakers.

Living only steps from Riverside Park, on this particularly quiet block of the Upper West Side, was definitely a perk. He warmed up at the 84th Street entrance before winding his way down to the running path that stretched all along the Hudson River. Heading south, he was up to his brisk eight-and-a-half minute per mile pace by the time he reached the Boat Basin at 79th Street. It was a gorgeous morning with all the cherry blossoms poised to burst at any moment.

Ordinarily, Preston would have been on the lookout to cruise other cute guys out running or cycling, but he was suddenly more mesmerized by the seasonal sights he was passing. There were not only the rosy buds of the cherry blossoms on every tree, but tulips, forsythia, and daffodils abounded to his left and the calm, glistening waters of the mighty Hudson shimmered to his right. Birds abounded, especially robins which were his mother's favorite seasonal harbinger. A gentle breeze at his back helped push him along, and he found himself humming some strange tune that seemed familiar but wasn't sure from where. The views were glorious, and he picked up his pace.

Unbeknownst to Preston, Milton was running, too. The miraculous rebirth of Spring surrounded them in all its dazzling color and fragrances. It reminded Milton of strolling along the Charles River Esplanade with his parents, but he had never experienced moving his body with such speed before, let alone so unfettered by constricting, starched clothing. He felt as if he were flying completely naked and the breeze tingled. When he'd gone into the sea water, it was the coldest sensation imaginable, but this coolness was refreshing. It was a heady sensation as everything whizzed by.

Preston, who for all his years of recreational running had never experienced the so-called "runner's high," suddenly became simultaneously exhilarated and somewhat aroused. He hoped to dart past some cute crotch-watchers who might appreciate the growing bulge in his shorts.

He overheard someone derisively call out "Faggot" and made a quick glance over his shoulder to see an overweight, red-faced man with a bushy mustache. He was clad in a white track suit with a NY Mets baseball cap on his head. Dismissing the jerk as someone who looked like he'd just climbed down from a tractor, Preston ignored the slur. Milton was reminded of the gymnasium steward Thomas McCawley. Even nowadays, he reckoned, there was plenty of prejudice to go around.

"Go, Yankees!" he called back, over his shoulder.

Preston's back kick sprang higher, and he leaned into his speed, accelerating as he continued to race through Hudson Yards, ever closer to the waterfront Chelsea Piers

Sports and Entertainment complex. At an average 5'10 but a lean 170 pounds, Preston cut an impressive athletic figure as his gait neared a sprint.

There was a huge ocean liner docked there, Cunard's flagship Queen Mary 2 from Southampton. It was a magnificent ship, more than a quarter longer than Titanic and twice as wide. In addition to her size, her single red funnel and sleek blue hull made her appear every bit as regal as her name. She was berthed at the Manhattan Cruise Terminal, less than two miles from the pier where Titanic had been scheduled to arrive more than a century earlier. Preston couldn't take his eyes off her.

His breathing suddenly arrested, and he flailed unexpectedly, instantly snapping out of his reverie to regain his footing and slow to a stop. Such a physical reaction had never happened to him before and he gasped for air, concerned. He tried briefly to walk it out but was forced to stop completely, wheezed as he bent over, and placed his hands on his quads while he recovered. He deduced that he had gotten carried away with the jubilation of his run.

When he finally straightened up and was able to catch his breath again, it was Milton's eyes that were fixated upon the massive structure of the vessel before them. It was a combination of awe and fear that kept Preston's heartbeat elevated. Queen Mary, along with her husband King George V, had been crowned the year before Titanic sailed. Was this ship named in her honor, he asked himself. If so, what had happened to "Queen Mary One?" Had she gone to the ocean floor like Titanic?

About two miles from home, Preston decided to turn around and walk back rather than risk another strange cardiovascular episode. He felt almost immediately better once he turned away from the ocean liner and was able to stride his way northward once again with ease. Still, it had been a bit of a scare for him and he decided, especially with all the thoughts of his thirtieth, he should make a doctor's appointment for a physical. It had been well over a year since his last examination, but he told himself it was some kind of anomaly. He was too young for any serious problems. He'd never even had Covid!

After a shower, he felt back to normal and tried to put the incident out of his mind. Drying off, he took a long, admiring look at his naked self in the full-length mirror on the back of the bathroom door. He clinically inspected the reflection from head to toe with vain efficiency.

His haircut was longish but sexy and his sideburns a perfect length. He had recently clipped his chest hair short enough to show off the definition of his pecs while still proving that he possessed the follicles to please any fur-loving gays. A "treasure trail" of light, soft hair led down to his pelvic area. He didn't quite have an abdominal six-pack, but he was working on it and still cut a lean, impressive figure. His neatly trimmed bush of pubic hair framed his genitals in a way that pleased Preston to see in the mirror. It even made him twitch a little with erotic pride. He was average-sized but quite satisfied with what nature had given him and always considered himself "a grower, not a shower."

His gaze continued down his long, muscular runner's legs all the way to his size 10.5 feet. Maybe he could use a pedicure, he conceded.

Milton looked on appreciatively, too, but finally decided it was time for Preston to move on and get dressed. But like Narcissus gazing at himself, Preston was too rapt to be moved. He was becoming more aroused by the sight of his own nakedness and sat down on the lid of the toilet seat, opposite, and began to fondle himself.

In life, Milton had not been immune to the experience of self-pleasure, but he derived no excitement from seeing it from Preston's point of view, and he attempted to disconnect from the observance.

As Preston's excitement mounted, he reached for a pump bottle of coconut oil lubricant that was on a low shelf behind the toilet. He was enjoying the show he was putting on for himself in the mirror. Climax impending, he grabbed a small red and yellow labeled brown bottle off the same shelf. "Rush," an amyl nitrate inhalant popular in the gay community for providing an intense but brief high, accentuated orgasm, and Preston took two long hits of the vapor. He immediately felt the subsequent euphoric head rush and hardened further, bringing Milton forward again.

While the increased heart rate and blood flow provided him an enhanced sexual experience, it produced a confusion bordering on panic for Milton. This new existence was already other-worldly but this beautiful, foreign body he now inhabited was rattling them into an altered, frightening state.

The result sent Preston's blood pressure soaring, even higher than the momentary experience he'd had earlier while running. It wasn't the usual "popper" huffing high, either. His head throbbed and the pounding was so intense, he lost his erection, and Preston bent over to hold his head in his hands, hoping it would stop. He broke out in a sudden, soaking cold sweat and closed his eyes tightly to attempt regulating his breath. He reminded Milton of a panting dog.

It took a few minutes, but the effects gradually subsided leaving Milton relieved and Preston shaken.

Still naked, he walked unsteadily to the kitchen and poured himself a glass of cold filtered water. Something was off. What couldn't he shake, he asked himself. He retrieved his phone and looked up the number to call his General Practitioner. A friendly receptionist answered after he went through the usual rigamarole of the automated recording whose "menu options had recently changed." They never changed, but he still had to wait to be prompted to press "3" to make an appointment.

"Manhattan Medical, this is Joanie speaking, how may I help you?"

"Hi, I'd like to come in for a routine physical. My name is Preston Spaulding."

"So I may find your records, what is your date of birth, Milton?"

"Preston. Preston Spaulding. October 19, 1994."

After hearing her press a few keystrokes on her laptop, she located his records and went through the protocol of scheduling the appointment for the following week. He felt reassured that he was being proactive.

Just as he was ending the call, he received a Facetime call from Greg. He went back to the bathroom and wrapped a towel around his waist before he answered and saw his best friend's cute, friendly face staring back at him from his Park Avenue office.

"Hey, doll. Happy hour at ReBar? I'm feeling the Chelsea vibe."

Preston quickly replied, "How about a healthy dinner at Cookshop instead? I could use a bit of a detox."

Cookshop was in that neighborhood, had a solid dinner menu, a festive atmosphere and, best of all, an adorable staff and clientele mainly comprised of gay men.

"If you insist. Marcus will try to meet us there if he gets off work in time." It was an easy walk from where Preston would be meeting his voice coach in nearby Greenwich Village.

Preston got through his singing lesson in good form, although the mysterious anxiety attacks remained of concern to him. He took his time strolling the elevated High Line Park, crowded with people enjoying the mild weather. He arrived at the restaurant to find Greg already seated a table sipping a cocktail while waiting.

He was suspicious when Preston only asked for a soft drink but after they ordered their meals, Greg demanded answers.

"Okay, what the hell is going on? Fish?" Greg asked his bestie of many years after Preston placed his dinner order for grilled salmon with hollandaise dressing on the side and extra steamed vegetables. They were both devotees of Cookshop's renowned Pork Chops and never ordered anything else.

"We work out like Olympians, so sue me if I'm trying to be more diligent with my diet, as well. I shouldn't have asked for the hollandaise, but I'm craving it for some reason."

It was Milton's favorite and the last meal he had aboard Titanic.

"And happy hour wasn't even mediocre hour. Is there something you're not telling me, Press?"

"You're the one who keeps harping on about my thirtieth," Preston defended. "Maybe I'm just thinking it's time to clean up my act."

"I want to plan a party, not start you on Hospice care."

Resisting the urge to grab a piece of bread from the basket a cute bus boy had just delivered to the table, Preston admitted, "I just don't feel like myself. I made an appointment for a physical."

Concerned, Greg turned suddenly more serious and leaned in, putting his elbows up on the tabletop. "What do you think it is?"

"Probably psychological. I was out dancing last night, the usual scene. It just suddenly all seemed so...pointless."

"I think you look fantastic. We both do. We're lucky. Men get more handsome with age."

"Not about my looks, stupid," Preston snapped back with good humor. "And get your elbows off the table!"

Obliging, Greg said, "Look, Miss Manners, if you're entering your prudish phase, I'm not going to put up with it. You don't have to be the Whore of Babylon, but you can't let yourself swing too far in the other direction, either. Look at Marcus and me."

"Yes, look at Marcus and you," he parroted, instantly realizing how snarky it sounded.

"I've seen you roll home after sunrise, walking with a limp, honey. Don't get all judgy. Marcus and I have been together for two years, and we still have fun."

"I know, I'm sorry. But looking the other way for a one-night stand or having the occasional three-way doesn't sound like much fun to me."

"It used to," his friend replied, defensively.

Preston considered for a moment and then acquiesced. "Yes. It used to."

Chapter Three

Preston sat uncomfortably on the papered examining table, trying to keep the flimsy gown closed around him while he waited for the doctor to come in. He was still thinking about the dream he'd had overnight. It struck him as unusual because he wasn't prone to dreams. Perhaps, he thought, it was because he'd abstained from any alcohol the night before knowing he would be having routine blood work at his physical.

In his dream, he was a boy again on his family's large estate in Chester County, Pennsylvania, a suburb of Philadelphia. The entire property was a kid's fantasy play world for an only child; from the barn and rolling fields to tree houses and an orchard, a large swimming pond and a gazebo. It was where he developed and cultivated a rich imaginary life of make-believe and play-acting. While his father may have hoped for him to follow in his footsteps as a businessman, his adoring mother was so certain Preston was destined to be an actor that she took him for his first audition at a local community theater when he was only 8 years of age. Her intuition proved correct when he landed the major role of John Darling in their production of *Peter and Wendy,* based on the classic Disney version of the *Peter Pan* story.

Even though his parents had sold the property and moved them into the town of West Chester, Preston vividly remembered almost every detail of the farm and his first eleven years there. In their large, three-story stone house atop the hill on Green Tree Avenue, young Preston played out a wide range of boyhood activities like building pillow forts, conducting amateur science experiments, and constructing elaborate model train sets. He almost never ran down the long flights of steps; it was much more fun to slide down the long wooden banisters.

The dream that invaded his sleep all night hadn't kept him awake, although he remembered it vividly. He would climb onto the banister and make the slide downstairs, but instead of ever reaching the bottom, he would just continue sliding endlessly into darkness. An eternal ride down, down, down. Did it mean anything or was it just a subconscious twist on a childhood memory?

He was still thinking about it when Dr. Lee entered the room, a serious physician specializing in gay men's health and HIV medicine. Even though the Covid pandemic was long over, Dr. Lee still always wore a mask in the office.

"It's about time you came in for a checkup," he said, his eyes glancing over Preston's chart. "An annual physical is defined as once every twelve months."

"Time flies when you're having fun," was the excuse Preston offered.

"I assume that means we should include an HIV test in your blood work. Any changes in your health?"

Anything that smacked of a guilt trip made Preston defensive. "I had a little shortness of breath while I was running, but otherwise I feel great. And, for the record, I always practice safe sex. I guess I'm just getting paranoid about turning thirty this year."

Dr. Lee looked at him, and it was disconcerting for Preston, who couldn't tell whether or not he was smiling underneath the mask.

"Life begins at forty, I have found. But I'm glad you're being proactive. You may want to consider a prescription for PrEP." As if reading from a pamphlet, he continued robotically, "That's the CDC recommended pill to help prevent HIV infection."

Preston knew all about PrEP. Most of the guys he knew were on it, but a few were never able to tolerate it without chronic nausea or diarrhea, so he preferred to stick with condoms and other safe sex practices.

There was a soft rap on the door before it opened and a good-looking young man in navy blue scrubs entered, wheeling in an EKG machine. Preston was certainly glad that he was maskless, and the two smiled at each other, an instant spark of attraction between them.

"Mr. Spaulding?" the hottie asked, having read the patient roster.

"This is Todd Hafkin, our new nurse practitioner. He'll be assisting with your lab tests."

"Nice to meet you," they both greeted in unison and then laughed because of it.

"You can call me Preston. Mr. Spaulding is my dad."

"I'll be back in shortly," Dr. Lee said, excusing himself so that Todd could perform his other duties of recording Preston's weight and blood pressure.

"Mind jumping on the scale for me?" Todd asked.

Careful to keep the skimpy cotton gown closed, Preston obliged and felt himself blush when Todd told him, "175. Absolutely perfect."

He returned to the table for his blood pressure check and cautioned, "It might be a little high. I guess I'm kind of nervous."

"That's called White Coat Syndrome," Todd told him with a smile. "Very normal for it to be slightly elevated in an office setting." Unexpectedly, he patted Preston on the shoulder, and suddenly Milton was there and could feel the same sensation as when Jack put his arm around his shoulder—instantaneous comfort.

"It's normal. Now you can stop being nervous."

"No, I can't. There's still the prostate exam."

Todd laughed easily and heartily, which Preston found extremely attractive.

"You still have a few years before you have to worry about that. Unless you just happen to want one?"

Preston looked at him, perplexed, but Todd quickly let him off the hook by adding, "Just kidding! I'll perform the EKG and take your blood."

For the electrocardiogram, Preston opened the gown to allow Todd to place the sticky electrodes on his chest. Preston and Milton both wondered if he was admiring the sight of his bare torso.

"Okay, just relax for a few minutes."

Preston closed his eyes while the test ran its course. In the resulting darkness, he could once again feel the descent down the banister, but it wasn't alarming. Rather, there was something so soothing and familiar about it that he could have easily dozed off if the EKG had lasted longer.

It was time to remove the electrodes, and Todd apologized if it caused any discomfort from the adhesive on his skin, adding, "Lucky you keep trimmed."

Preston smiled slyly. He had noticed.

The wholesome, smiling nurse practitioner stayed on Preston's mind for the rest of the day and it surprised him. If he had a "type," it wasn't Todd. He usually preferred beefier, brooding guys. In fact, he had a dinner date with one that very evening, a brawny chef named Dom. Now that he had been so instantly captivated at the doctor's office, he was regretting his plans. Greg often teased him, "Being fickle is one of your most attractive qualities."

Some friends have a knack for being guardian angels and Alanna Murray was that for Preston. He often referred to her as the big sister he'd never had. Just as he was trying to muster up enthusiasm for spending dinner (and quite likely a sleepover) with Dom, she sent him a text to ask if he wanted to hang out at her place that evening for a home cooked meal. It was the perfect excuse to wrangle out of his date, and he quickly typed out a message to Dom saying, "Sorry! Friend with a last-minute crisis. Can't make dinner. Reschedule soon. Preston."

He followed that with an immediate reply to Alanna saying to count him in. He was trading one talented chef for another.

She had been a casting director when he first moved to Manhattan and met her when he auditioned for an Off-Broadway show. He didn't land the part, but he made a new friend and confidant after they'd immediately hit it off after a spontaneous night of karaoke and tequila shots. She stroked his ego by being an ardent admirer of his looks and talent, and she was an amusing, reliable cohort for a night out or any social event where he benefitted from having an attractive woman on his arm. She ended up briefly doing some TV episodic casting on shows like *Law and Order* and *Blue Bloods* and would hire him for bit parts and day player roles, often telling him he was "too pretty" to play cops or villains and had to keep on the lookout for more suitable characters like models or real estate agents.

"I'm an actor," he would argue. "I can play anything!"

"Television doesn't care about your talent," she'd contend. "That's why they call it type-casting."

Even so, they developed a close friendship away from show business and stuck by each other through the ups and downs of failed love affairs and, most impactful,

Alanna's struggle for sobriety after some serious problems with drugs and alcohol. A prolonged stint in rehab seemed to have finally straightened her out, although she prided herself on being "a dry drunk" and able to keep all the best parts of her personality without chemical inducement.

For Preston, it was a pleasant change to abstain from drinking and "stay in" for a change, even though she never gave him any grief about partying. He loved Alanna's chic Upper East side co-op apartment that had been in her family for decades. It was exquisitely decorated in French Country style with lots of antiques and chic original details such as crown molding, white oak hardwood in parquet patterns, and glass paneled doors separating the rooms. It reeked of "old money" Manhattan-style as if she might have been a long-lost granddaughter of one of Truman Capote's "Swans."

She had made an enormous lasagna that was baking in the oven, and the tantalizing aroma made Preston's mouth water the moment he crossed the threshold, clutching an inexpensive bouquet of tulips he had impulsively purchased on his way across town.

After they greeted each other with a warm embrace, Alanna took the tulips and said, "I'll put these in water, and you can help me toss the salad. I hope you're hungry."

"For your lasagna, always."

"When you told me you had your physical today, I opted for a healthy version. Turkey instead of beef and low sodium."

"My blood pressure was fine, I'll have you know. And the hot male nurse told me my weight was perfect."

She teasingly told him, "You don't need anyone to tell you that. You already know you're perfect. Tell me about the nurse. Was he a Himbo?"

"Hunky yes, but smart and with a soft touch. Think of a Ken doll in scrubs. Not my usual type, but adorable and flirty."

"An added incentive to keep up with your health care. Bravo."

He washed his hands and proceeded to assist with the salad preparation.

"After dinner, let's watch an old movie. I've been binging disaster films like *The Towering Inferno* and *Earthquake.*

He jumped in with an immediate suggestion. "How about *The Poseidon Adventure*? I haven't seen that in years and it's one of my all-time favorites."

"Mine, too!"

The 1972 Irwin Allen all-star epic was about an ocean liner capsized by a rogue tidal wave, and the story followed a small band of survivors trying to make their escape from the upside-down hell of the stricken vessel. It was campy but compelling, filled with memorable performances from the likes of Gene Hackman, Roddy McDowall, Stella Stevens, and Shelley Winters.

During dinner, the friends caught up and Preston shared how infatuated he was with Todd. He also mentioned how suddenly he seemed to be losing interest in the promiscuous, party lifestyle pervasive among his peers in the gay community.

Alanna sweetly observed, "And here you are drinking sparkling water with me for a movie night. Maybe you're growing out of your Dorian Gray period."

"Is that what it is? Should I worry?"

"Even the wildest among us get more conservative with age," she continued. "Just please smack me if I ever say I'm going to Mar-a-Lago."

"I know the wholesome thing works for you, sweetie, but I have never been interested in giving up partying. I like it. I like recreational drugs. And casual sex. When have I ever talked about wanting to settle down?"

"You're too young to have a mid-life crisis, Preston. So, what is all this?"

"That's just it. I don't know. I thought I knew myself. I certainly liked myself and the way I was living my life. Even if my parents have issues with it."

"I've gone to enough therapists over the years to know it always comes back to the parents."

"My folks sent me to a child psychiatrist in the sixth grade because I was always talking to myself. That lasted exactly two sessions because I refused to open my mouth. If they didn't want me playing make-believe with imaginary friends, I sure as shit wasn't going to talk to a shrink."

She reached across the table and put her hand over his, smiling knowingly.

He reflexively withdrew his hand from her touch and instantly regretted it, not wanting to offend his dear friend.

"Maybe I just need to go out and get laid."

"Sweetie, maybe that's the last thing you need to do."

Preston was unused to being admonished or lectured and he was at a loss for words.

"You didn't know me back when I fucking any guy with a pulse. Fortunately, I was black-out drunk most of the time, so I don't remember most of them, myself."

"What's your point?"

"It was a downward spiral, but hitting the proverbial rock bottom ended up being the catalyst for me cleaning up my act once and for all."

Defensively, he snapped back, "Rock bottom?! Is that where you think I'm headed?"

Milton wanted Preston to hold his tongue and listen to this obviously wise and caring woman.

Patiently and with a light smile, Alanna said, "You're like family I got to choose for myself, Press. I just want you to take care of yourself. Because I'm selfish and I want you to be around forever."

"Maybe misery likes company, but I am not going to rehab."

She hadn't meant to hurt his feelings, so she immediately steered the subject elsewhere.

"No, you're going to have a second helping of lasagna, and then we're going to watch the movie. And maybe tomorrow you'll call that nurse and ask him out on a proper date."

With bellies full of lasagna, they began watching *The Poseidon Adventure* and Alanna mentioned that the early exterior scenes aboard the fictional liner were filmed aboard the Queen Mary in Long Beach, California, which was a floating tourist attraction she had once visited on a West

Coast business trip. Preston was now distracted from their dinner conversation, mesmerized with studying the actual ship's decks and funnels. She noticed his intense interest that seemed to rise above the almost comedic, campy aspect of the actors' dialogue.

"Thinking of taking a cruise?" she asked him, sarcastically.

"I should have paid more attention when my parents took me on a Cunard liner to Bermuda as a kid. Those stupid new amusement park mega-ships can't compare with beauties like that. I actually saw the Queen Mary 2 when it was docked here."

"I didn't know you were such a maritime enthusiast," she kidded.

"I wasn't. Maybe I'm becoming one."

Early into the film a giant tidal wave strikes the top-heavy Poseidon, and she rolls over in a dramatic scene where the cast is thrown around the Grand Dining Saloon, "killing off" several minor characters, extras and stunt people. It's one of the many exciting, well-shot moments of the motion picture, but rather than enjoying the spectacle, Preston sat on Alanna's sofa wide eyed and felt his heart begin to beat faster.

Milton was instantly at attention as they watched the ornate ship set turn on its head, and water suddenly came crashing in and swamping many who had been able to initially survive the capsize. The cries of the passengers were terrifying, and Preston's breath hitched as he stared at the TV screen, unblinking. It was startling when a special effects shot of the inverted Poseidon underwater depicted one of her boilers exploding. It caused Milton to gasp in recollection of the almost identical sound on Titanic. No sound was audible from Preston, but he felt the choke in his own breathing.

Alanna noticed and tentatively asked, "You okay?"

He waved at her to hush, and when the story moved to the next scene, as Gene Hackman and his fellow celebrity survivors began to assess their situation, Preston simply said, "I forgot how great this movie is." She wasn't as enthusiastic about it as her buddy, and she allowed herself to nod off.

By the end of the film, as the six sole survivors were rescued from the stricken vessel, Preston was still rapt. Alanna was sound asleep, which he didn't even notice until the closing credits began to roll. He gave her a gentle nudge and softly said, "I'm gonna head home. Thanks again for dinner and the movie." He was relieved not to have let their earlier discussion escalate into an argument; he knew she meant well.

They'd had movie nights and slumber parties before, so she was comfortable enough to let Preston see himself out. Groggy, she replied, "Turn off the TV for me. Talk to you tomorrow."

As he flipped off the television and stood up to leave she added, "And Press, don't sweat the small stuff."

He hailed a taxi heading back to the West side, just as a light rain began to fall. His phone told him it wasn't even eleven, and here he was already heading home to bed. On a Friday night in Manhattan! He still felt a sting of resentment from Alanna's rock-bottom reference. She didn't understand that he liked his life just as it was.

Preston always kept a couple ecstasy tablets in his wallet, "for emergency use only," and deemed this as a worthy occasion.

"Excuse me, could you drop me at 80th and Broadway instead, please?" he impulsively asked the driver as he fished out his wallet and popped one of the pills.

There was a small neighborhood adult bookstore, Bon Soir, that had existed on West 80th Street forever, best known by longtime local gay men as a place for a quick pickup. Greg had always joked that it should have been called "Desperate Measures." Once Preston got out of the cab, scurrying to the unobtrusive green entry door to avoid the rain, he fought off a nagging feeling inside him that he should skip it and just continue the four additional blocks to his apartment. Milton didn't like the look of this place. He somehow knew what was on the other side of that green door and didn't want to go inside.

Preston suppressed the indecision as the molly's effects began to kick in and pressed the intercom buzzer to be admitted into Bon Soir. Milton disappeared.

He climbed two flights of rickety, unswept stairs to reach the entry door. Inside, behind a glass partition that looked insubstantial to provide any real protection, was a heavy set, wheezing old queen who collected the twenty dollar "cash only" admission fee through a slot.

From there, Preston walked through one of a pair of subway-style turnstiles, leading to a series of "peep show" rooms and some other cheaply constructed "cabanas" where patrons could engage in their choice of casual, anonymous sex acts. Old disco music from a bygone era played throughout the establishment, and the entire facility was bathed in a dim, pinkish glow from the neon lighting.

Preston wandered along the hallway, glancing into each room to check out if there was anyone interesting but only managed to observe a few rather tragic-looking mature gentlemen.

"God, shoot me first," he said to himself, vowing never to become an old gay man.

He came upon two younger men leaning against a wall, locked in a clinch with their wide-open mouths pressed together. Across from them was a buff young man with muscles that seemed to burst out of his tight t-shirt. In the psychedelic haze that had come over him from the drugs, he wasn't sure if it was Dom. The guy had the same ebony hair and a permanent five o'clock shadow, like a walking Tom of Finland illustration.

The hirsute hulk beckoned him with a surly head cock and Preston instinctively moved over to him. They began to make out and, without a moment's hesitation, the man roughly grabbed Preston's crotch, making him wince in surprise and pain.

"Hey, easy does it," Preston loudly whispered even as they continued to kiss. The protestation only made the brute more feverishly aggressive, and he kept his hand pressed forcibly against Preston's groin. The scent of a familiar cologne mingled with sweat and whatever ammonia-based cleaner Bon Soir used, causing his dinner to repeat itself in his stomach, sickeningly.

He was so fucked up, he thought he heard the man saying through gnashed teeth, "I thought you couldn't get together tonight."

Preston squirmed. He was further turned off when the man took his other hand and used it to push down on the top of Preston's head. His immediate thought was for his hair, but then he found himself being powerfully pushed down onto his knees. He'd had rough sex before and wasn't surprised to encounter it here, so he initially went along with it. But his head was then being shoved toward the guy's genitals, which Preston hadn't realized were exposed through his open jeans. The fat, veiny phallus he thought he recognized as Dom's was only inches away.

The rough hand moved to grab his cock and force himself to Preston's mouth, ill-equipped to handle the girth and pressure with which it was being thrust. He coughed and sputtered.

"Take it, bitch," came a command from overhead.

Preston gagged some more, futilely attempting to accommodate the oral pounding he was receiving. He could feel his eyes watering, and thought he might vomit at any second.

From somewhere, the man pulled out a small vial of poppers and held them against Preston's nostril to take a huff. As soon as he detected the familiar aroma of the solvent, Preston felt as if Alanna's lasagna was about to make a reappearance. He vigorously pushed the hand away and quickly got to his feet and staggered away.

"Pathetic fag," Preston heard from behind him as he briskly stepped out of the room to head for home.

The banister dream would come to him again that night, even if he didn't remember it in the morning.

⚝ ⚝ ⚝

Milton had managed to disengage from Preston's distasteful behavior, but this brutal development jolted him back to attention because of its frightening familiarity.

It had been just after he enrolled at Columbia University as a freshman in the Class of 1905. No sooner had he been swept up in the exhilaration of leaving his comparatively sleepy suburban existence outside of Springfield, Massachusetts, for the metropolitan environs of Manhattan, than he'd been confronted with his first sexually charged encounter. After an intimate moment with an older man Milton had dared to trust, he was cajoled into meeting in a dark and secluded spot in the back of the Low Memorial

Library. It was late in the evening, and the building was almost completely deserted, save for a drowsy librarian at the front entrance desk. It was soon to close until the next day, but the man had lured him there with a confidence that told Milton he certainly knew where they could find complete privacy.

They had eyed each other earlier in the day on Hamilton Lawn, the man offering Milton a seductive glance that was unmistakably flirtation. Against his better instincts, Milton reflexively slowed his walking pace to a stroll so that the dapper-looking man of about thirty-five could make his way over in a seemingly casual fashion. He was auburn-haired and had an impeccably groomed and waxed mustache over his sensual lips.

"Mind if I walk with you?" he asked Milton in almost a whisper.

Milton's heart was pounding in his chest, and he could also feel his loins stirring in a thrilling way he'd never experienced before. He managed to find enough breath to reply, "With pleasure."

The pair continued to amble side by side, their eyes instinctively kept straight ahead to maintain an air of propriety in spite of their instant, mutual attraction. Milton used his peripheral vision to try and get a better look at his new companion. He could see that his European-style navy blue suit was accessorized with a brighter blue pocket square.

Some other pedestrians, three women, were walking toward them, so the men politely began to veer to the right of the pavement to allow the ladies to pass . As they did so, the man accidentally brushed his arm against Milton's, which instantly gave the young man a spontaneous erection.

With his gaze still fixed ahead and not on Milton, the man quietly asked, "Would you care to meet me this evening at the Low Library?"

Milton was unsure of how to respond, especially as it was entirely possible he was misunderstanding the man's intentions. He stopped walking, and his acquaintance did so as well. Milton turned his head to look the man directly in the face and noticed that, while rather ordinary looking, he possessed an erotic and mysterious flair.

All Milton could think to say was, "What time?"

Adopting a nonchalant air, the man answered, "Eight thirty. In the rear stacks, in between African Studies and Taxidermy."

Before Milton spoke further, the man turned and walked away from him, now with a quicker pace, so that he was soon far ahead. He turned a corner as he neared the newly unveiled Alma Mater statue and disappeared. Milton swallowed hard before checking his monogrammed pocket watch that told him it was just past four in the afternoon. He had just over four hours to decide against the rendezvous, but he desperately wanted to give in to the temptation and hoped the stranger would also stay true to his word.

At precisely eight twenty-eight, according to his watch, Milton was seated on a wrought iron bench across from the library, dimly lit by the Weisbach Gas lights that lined the street. The temperature had plummeted unexpectedly as the sun set, and it was unseasonably cold enough that Milton could even see his breath. He didn't mind the cold, but nonetheless folded his arms across his chest to try and warm himself. If he was shivering, it was more because of nervousness than the chill in the air. There were very few people around, and he hadn't noticed anyone going in or out of the library's entry doors. He managed to stay seated for another minute before taking a deep inhale to help summon his courage. He tried to look casual as he made his way to the steps of the building and hoped no one would notice him as he moved inside.

After a perfunctory nod to the nonplussed desk librarian, Milton began to walk purposefully to the rear stacks, as he had been directed. His pulse was racing with a heady blend of thrill and fear, hoping it didn't show. He could see labels on shelf ends and kept an eye out for "African Studies," trying to act as if he knew precisely where he was going and which books he was looking for.

Sure enough, he could see ahead that "Taxidermy" was at the very end of the long row and virtually in complete darkness. But there was no sign of the man who had invited him there.

Milton felt deflated and questioned whether or not he should be feeling humiliated as well. He stood there for a moment, telling himself he had been foolish to want to take such a risk in the first place and what his parents would think of his reckless behavior.

As he turned to walk out of the dark canyon of bookshelves, the strange man stepped out from behind one of the rows, directly in Milton's path. His bright blue pocket square was the only color that seemed to stand out in the shadows. Neither of them spoke as they came face to face, only inches apart. Milton's nostrils were filled with the intermingled scent of his own perspiration and the man's musky after-shave lotion.

He took Milton by the hand and led him into the further darkness of the long corridor of bookshelves. There was no going back now.

The man gently moved in to bring his face a hair's breadth away from Milton's cheek. Milton remained stone-still to allow the man the opportunity to lead the way through this encounter. The mustache, which he'd noticed had been so perfectly styled, brushed against his cheek causing a tantalizing rush of anticipation and delight inside Milton, causing his own lips to part in anticipation of a kiss.

Instead, the man had raised a small glass vial up toward Milton's nose. "Sniff this," he said firmly in a whisper.

Even in the barely lit, isolated space Milton could see that there was some sort of powdered contents in the vial. Cocaine, he assumed. Once favored by the upper class, the substance was now thought of as the favored drug of prostitutes, gamblers, and bohemians. Even the Coca-Cola company has recently stopped using it in the soft drink formula.

Milton turned his head away and whispered back, "No, thank you."

It hadn't been a request. The vial was again thrust in the direction of Milton's nostrils, more forcefully, and the man pushed against him strong enough that Milton felt his back pressed up against the bookshelf.

Trying to utter "no" again, the word caught in Milton's throat. The vial disappeared back into the man's pocket, and he now clutched Milton's arms with such power that the frightened young student could only freeze in place, lest he make a commotion that would surely draw attention to their tryst. The stimulation of the liaison had quickly changed to one of fear. Milton had never been manhandled in such a fashion.

Milton could discern rage in the man's face and was surprised by his strength. Was he a "Jack the Ripper," about to pull out a knife? Milton's mind raced to decide if he should succumb or fight back. Either option was sure to have a bad outcome.

"Attention, attention," a feeble voice from somewhere nearby suddenly called out to no one in particular. "The Library will soon be closing for the night."

The men locked eyes in a flash of mutual silence. It lasted only a second or two, but it seemed to linger endlessly until the man resolved to satisfy his carnal urge. Pressing his body fully against Milton, pinned to the bookshelf, he began quickly thrusting into him. Milton squeezed his eyes tightly closed in a useless attempt at ignoring what was happening.

The man continued to grind himself wildly against Milton's leg. Keeping as quiet as possible, Milton could still hear the labored, heavy breathing of his attacker as he became more and more aroused. There was no such stimulation for Milton.

In less than a minute, it was clear that the man had reached a climax, and he emitted a low, primal grunt in the process then immediately pulled back and away from Milton, releasing his grip. Milton allowed his eyes to open in time to see him straighten his jacket and tie before turning away and walking off at a quick, clipped pace.

Milton was left standing there, shaken, and could hear the heels of the man's shoes clicking on the tiled floors as he moved further and further off toward the exit.

"Closing in five minutes," the librarian's voice echoed.

Milton fled the stacks almost as quickly as he would then depart Columbia and abandon his studies there, before they'd even really begun in earnest.

He promised himself to forever wipe the incident from his memory and had successfully repressed it until this moment with Preston.

※※※

Dr. Lee's office emailed Preston the results of his blood work, and everything came back normal. It was always a relief to get a clean bill of health, especially about HIV and STDs, but Dr. Lee had included an advisory to "keep an eye on blood pressure," and it got him thinking again about Todd, the nurse practitioner who'd performed the test.

Since he probably wouldn't be back to the office again until next year's physical, Preston reasoned it would be okay to take Alanna's advice and reach out in an attempt to ask Todd out for a date. He struggled to recall Todd's surname and went onto the website of Dr. Lee's practice to track it down.

It was easy. There he was, Todd Hafkin, NP. There was even a photograph of him, all smiles, with his short, sandy hair and adorable ears that stuck out to make him look even more boyish. There was a short biography that reported Todd had obtained his undergraduate degree from NYU and graduate degree from Columbia University before completing internships in internal medicine and infectious disease. It also noted that "Mr. Hafkin's interests include literature, classic films and snowboarding."

Snowboarding? Preston didn't know any gay men in the City who snowboarded. Was his gaydar so off that he might have been mistaken about Todd's sexuality?

In the name of research, he jumped onto his Instagram account and searched for Todd there. Bingo. His profile picture was the same image used on Dr. Lee's website. He only had a few hundred followers and hadn't posted much content aside from some standard shots of special desserts, spectacular sunsets, a trip to a ski lodge, and several of an overweight cat that was apparently named Arnold Palmer. Not even a single thirst trap. No real clues to be found here.

Preston clicked on the "Follow" tab of Todd's account and then decided to send him a Direct Message. He'd be sure to keep it safely generic and considered for a few minutes before writing, "Got my lab results back, all good. Thanks for taking care of me. Reach out if you ever want to see a movie. Preston Spaulding."

A movie seemed like a reasonable proposal, given the mini biography. "Literature and skiing" didn't provide much first date opportunity. Now he'd just have to wait and see if Todd would respond.

To his delight, by the next time Preston checked his social media feeds, there was already a reply from Todd. It was appropriately professional and discreet, but also with an enthusiastic air that seemed indicative of his personality.

"Great to hear from you! I'm a member of the IFC if you like old movies. Message me and we'll make a plan."

Preston was psyched. The Independent Film Center occupied the space of the extensively renovated historic Waverly theater in Greenwich Village, and there were plenty of places to grab a drink before or after a film. He quickly sent Todd a response, suggesting available dates in the coming weeks.

Of all the revival art houses in New York City, Preston and Todd landed on a date night when the award-winning 1958 British film *A Night to Remember* was playing as part of a double bill at the Waverly. It was an acclaimed docudrama adaptation of Walter Lord's book of the same name, and one of the more historically accurate depictions of the Titanic tragedy. Preston had caught James Cameron's version on TV a few times over the years but having enjoyed seeing *The Poseidon Adventure* at Alanna's made him interested in this one. It would be a bonus to sit beside Todd in the darkened theater.

When the two men rendezvoused on West 3rd Street, they noticed on the Waverly's marquee what the second film would be 1953's soapy version with Barbara Stanwyck and Robert Wagner, simply entitled *Titanic.*

"Don't worry," Todd assured him with a laugh. "We don't have to stay for both."

After Preston bought them sodas from the concessions stand, they settled into their seats inside the charming old cinema. *A Night to Remember* was gripping from the first scene and seemed to perfectly capture the feeling and experience of life aboard the ship, as well as the Edwardian code of honor, evident especially among members of the social elite. Milton concurred and watched along, spellbound, as the hero of this version, Second Officer Charles Lightoller, rescued as many passengers as he could before the ship took its final plunge.

Somewhere around the point where Margaret "Molly" Brown took the oars of Lifeboat Number 6, Todd finally put his hand on Preston's thigh. It was an exciting moment in the climax of the film and felt like the right time to make a physical move. Preston, however, was so caught up in what was unfolding on screen that he didn't even notice. What he did notice was an unsettling sense of déjà vu.

His eyes darted around the chaotic scenes of stranded passengers scrambling to somehow rescue themselves. He was searching their faces while Milton was asking, where is Jack?

The final scene depicts Lightoller aboard the rescue ship Carpathia, discussing the staggering loss of life as debris floats by, underscored by a sad, stoic orchestral soundtrack. The final shot is of a Titanic life ring in the water.

The house lights in the theater came up, and most of the audience members began to stand and depart. It was then that Preston noticed Todd's hand, and he turned to him and smiled, feeling somehow exhausted by the film, as if he had lived through the experience along with the characters.

"That was really something," was all he could say.

Todd gave his leg a bit of a squeeze and smiled back before saying, "Let's go grab some dinner. What are you in the mood for?"

Preston noticed an older couple sitting in front of them, pulling out a plastic bag from which they retrieved some sandwiches and bottled water. They were obviously staying for the second feature.

"Why don't we stay?" Preston ventured.

"You want another two hours of Titanic?!" Todd asked, surprised.

"We can have a picnic right here. My treat."

The IFC had an adjacent restaurant with a full bar called Great Performances which served dinner and Todd shrugged, "If you're really that into it…"

"It's been so long since I've seen anything on the big screen, and don't you want to see how the two movies compare?"

Todd moved his hand higher up Preston's leg and leaned in to ask, provocatively, "If we stay for the next one, do I get an invitation back to your place afterwards?"

Preston felt instantly aroused by his confident but tender touch, so unlike the asshole who shoved him around at Bon Soir. He still hadn't figured out if it had actually been Dom, even as familiar as that cock had appeared, and he was certainly too mortified to call him and find out. Preston moved his face closer to Todd's and answered, "You have a deal."

They shared a sweet, short kiss that confirmed the mutual attraction they felt for each other.

"Come on, let's hurry," Preston said before he let himself get further carried away with his physical impulse. They rushed off to have a quick intermission meal.

By the time they returned to their seats, the theater lights had already dimmed, and the iconic 20th Century Fox fanfare was signaling the start of the feature. They had just shared an order of fish and chips in the restaurant, washed down with cold beers and were now in a jovial mood to huddle together.

Preston was unprepared for the shock of the film's very first image, archival footage of an actual massive iceberg, breaking apart and settling into its position where it would eventually contact and destroy the Titanic. Sol Kaplan's dramatic score was loud and terrifying.

Even though this version of the Titanic tragedy at times bordered on melodrama, with Stanwyck's character bantering with her prudish estranged husband, played by Clifton Webb, the special effects were top-notch for their time, and Preston once again became entranced. Todd noticed and simply thought it was endearing.

When Robert Wagner first appeared on screen, as a fictional character named Gifford, Milton sprung to immediate attention. He looked a great deal like Jack and was about the same age. Gifford managed to survive.

Handsomely distinguished actor Brian Aherne was almost a twin for Captain Smith, Preston thought, although he didn't understand why.

Todd put his arm around Preston, and they pressed their torsos together as cozily as they could in the confines of their seats. Milton felt comforted by it, just as he had when Jack had put his arm around him on the deck as they made their way to the rising stern.

On screen, the doomed passengers sang "Nearer My God to Thee" as they faced their imminent, inevitable fate. It was an emotionally impactful moment, but Preston quietly observed, "That's not right." Thanks to Hollywood screenwriters, even Jewish Isidor and Ida Straus were singing along with the hymn.

Suddenly, before the final strains of what would be their requiem, a terrific explosion seemingly came out of nowhere, interrupting the momentary serenity and rocked the set, sending everyone flying. The excellent model replica of Titanic began a rapid descent into the churning water.

Milton gasped so loudly, shocked and upset, that it escaped through Preston's mouth and startled Todd in the process. While only a minute and half more remained of the final scene, Preston could barely manage to sit still. He gulped at the air to catch his breath. Milton could see the reproduction of the ship's railing onto which he had clung futilely. It was horrifying to relive, and Preston trembled, still huffing and puffing.

Todd grabbed him firmly to steady him and whispered with the calm, concerned reassurance of a medical professional, "Deep breaths. Take it easy."

Mercifully, the scene quickly shifted to a final shot of lifeboats rowing past icebergs in the first light of dawn and a narrator calmly reported, "Thus on April the 15th, 1912, at 02:20 hours, RMS Titanic sank beneath the icy waves of the North Atlantic taking with her 1,514 men, women and children. 710 people, in 20 lifeboats, survived."

The house lights were coming up and, other than the older couple in front of them, they were the only remaining people left in the audience. Preston was still breathing heavily as Todd stroked his arm, reassuringly, and said, "Steady now, you're okay. It's just a movie."

"No. No, it's not."

Innately, Preston knew he had been there. On Titanic.

Todd had walked them out of the theater and around the corner to a little neighborhood bar, where he ordered them a nightcap of vodka tonics. Preston was embarrassed by his

outburst and apologized for it adding, "You won't want a second date with me after this."

"We'll see a Disney movie next time," Todd replied, good-naturedly. "Besides, our first date isn't over yet. You promised me I could come over."

"You don't think I'm ready for a straitjacket?"

"That's another movie altogether. Joan Crawford, if I remember correctly."

"I've never been one for metaphysical shit. But I honestly felt a connection with the sinking of that ship."

"Who's to say? Maybe you just have a lot of empathy. I've been known to cry at movies from time to time."

"It wasn't empathy. I've studied acting enough to know how to inhabit a character. This felt more like...an actual memory."

Again, Preston felt self-conscious. Especially saying this aloud to someone whose profession was rooted in science. He tried to brush it off by saying, "Maybe I have an overactive imagination."

Todd put his hand over Preston's in a supportive, tender gesture. "Not everything can be explained."

Preston was grateful for his tolerance. This certainly wasn't normal first date fare, and he wanted to show his appreciation for it.

"Let's forget about the Titanic and get back to my place," Preston suggested, squeezing his hand.

Todd smiled and called an Uber.

It took almost no time for the men to tumble into Preston's bed and remove each other's clothing in between deep, voracious kisses. Even though it was their first moment of sexual connection, they had a rapport and easy synchronicity. It was as if each man already knew precisely what would please and entice their partner.

The attractive young nurse was a skilled and generous lover and their coming together felt unusually romantic, especially considering they'd had no real courtship leading up to it. As Todd wrapped his arms tightly around him, Preston realized he was experiencing sex in a new way. The animalistic, primal urges of his previous, party-fueled escapades were not present. Being in bed with Todd was like a gentle dance back and forth in rhythm with each other.

It allowed Milton to feel it, too. Drinking in the sensations, scents, and sounds of two men making love, he believed that this is what it could or would have been like had he ever had the chance to be with Jack.

Chapter Four

Todd slipped out early the next morning, whispering to Preston that he had to get home to feed his cat, Arnold Palmer, and get ready for work. Preston didn't let on that he already knew the cat's name.

"Call me," Todd said, giving him an affectionate peck on the forehead.

Preston glanced at his phone, which told him it was just six oh-one in the morning, so he rolled back over to get some more sleep. All he had on his schedule was to film a self-tape audition for a day player role on a TV series, *The Equalizer*.

Milton stirred along with him and thought about how much he liked Todd. There was a lot that reminded him of Jack and not just physically. Todd's spirit and energy were light and positive, compassionatereword. Nursing was certainly an admirable vocation for someone with those qualities, even though Milton had never known of a male in that profession. Modern times seemed to be full of amazing liberties.

As Preston slept, Milton thought about the two similar sinking scenes in the movie versions of Titanic. He had missed the sight of the final plunge in reality, but those startling reenactments clearly showed that the ship had slipped under the waves in one piece. Had Jack made it off as he had planned by leaping away from the ship and into the water? Could he have possibly survived in the freezing sea until a lifeboat retrieved him? In this age of seemingly boundless information, he somehow knew that all would ultimately be revealed to him. And to Preston.

Patience. After all, it's not like he was going anywhere.

Preston, however, felt the floodgates of Titanic mania open wide once he got out of bed and had his first cup of coffee. Dozens of indelible images from the double feature ran through his mind: from the polite society behavior of first class and the rollicking optimism of the third-class immigrants, to the heartbreaking farewell scenes of families split apart as the lifeboats launched, and the sheer horror of being left to drown in the freezing black of night.

Still in his boxer shorts and a tee shirt, Preston turned on the television and brewed a second cup of coffee. Instead of his usual morning local news fare, he searched for James Cameron's 1997 *Titanic* film and decided to watch it right then. It had been years since he'd seen it. He wouldn't move for another three hours and fifteen minutes.

The contrived love story of the fictional Jack Dawson and Rose DeWitt Bukater, played by Leonardo DiCaprio and Kate Winslet, captivated him less than the breathtaking details of the period costumes, sets, and special effects—all in glorious color, unlike the movies he'd seen at the Waverly. The exquisite James Horner soundtrack enhanced the drama, especially once the iceberg and Titanic finally made contact. Two male extras playfully kicked chunks of ice around the deck, unaware of their peril ahead.

Who were those men supposed to be, Preston wondered. Did he have a connection with one of them?

In the film's most startling scene, when Titanic is agonizingly torn in half and momentarily eases back into the water before filling up with water and being dragged to her demise, Preston could again feel his pulse begin to pound. He was glued to the images, even as horrifying as they were to watch. It was a miracle anyone survived at all.

So much for the belief that the vessel had gone down in one piece. This depiction of her final moments was more violent and chaotic than what they had watched the night before. Milton saw no sign of the "real" Jack, his friend John Borland Thayer III, but he was encouraged that Preston was developing such an interest in the story. He wondered if

Preston would probe further into the history and uncover some answers.

By the time the movie ended, the entire morning was gone and Preston hurried to shower and get down to the business of preparing his audition. Even as he taped the scene in which he portrayed a distraught young man on the phone with a 911 operator, calling to report a gruesome crime, he found himself rushing through it, so he could get back to poking around to learn more about Titanic and what possible liaison there could be for him.

He emailed *The Equalizer* clip to his agent, then to be forwarded to the casting director, but he knew damned well it wasn't his best work and tried not to care. He made himself a sandwich and sat down at his laptop. He closed the two open browser windows, one to an adult film site he frequented for jerk off incentives and another to OpenTable, his go-to outlet for restaurant reservations. To try and understand his connection to "the ship of dreams" would require quite literally a deep dive.

The amount of information was so overwhelming, Preston pulled out notepaper and a pen to jot down notes as he Googled his way. In addition to all the motion pictures, there were TV movies, mini-series, stage plays, musicals, and scores of documentaries. If he wanted to read about the disaster, there was no end to the number of books and websites on the subject, written from 1912 right up to the present day. Kids' books, coloring books, cookbooks, diaries, biographies, dramatizations, encyclopedias and novels. There were historical societies, enthusiast groups, conventions, podcasts. Serious historical scholars and scientific explorers abounded, right alongside Cos players and film fans. Virtual tours of the ship as she looked in 1912 and to the deep-sea wreck, as she looked in the present. Anything, even remotely Titanic-related, was met with more than enthusiasm or fascination; it was fanaticism. One podcast proudly referred to their family of fans as "Titaniacs."

The afternoon flew by without Preston ever leaving his computer. He didn't know exactly what he was looking for, just that there was some personal connection to Titanic's story he had to find. He ordered two books on Amazon and subscribed to a podcast. He questioned why he'd never been bitten by this particular bug before, although it was certainly a far cry from the campier genres his community favored, such as John Waters films, *Mommie Dearest* or *RuPaul's Drag Race*.

He finally looked up from the screen when a text came in from Greg asking if he was free to meet up for happy hour. His friend had included a candid photo he'd taken on the subway of some random cute guy, a ritual they shared with each other whenever they could sneak a cheeky shot of someone they thought the other would find hot. This fellow definitely had Preston written all over him, at least as Greg knew his type to be: tall, dark, broad, clad in a skin-tight tank top and butt-hugging jeans.

"Mmm, not bad," Preston admitted.

Milton wanted him to put the phone down and get back to the computer screen, but Preston's libido won out.

"Been locked in the apartment all day," Preston replied. "Tiki Chick 6pm?"

Tiki Chick was a bustling Upper West Side joint near his apartment on Amsterdam Avenue, always crowded with a mix of young cosmopolitan men and women of assorted persuasions. Preston knew Greg would have preferred someplace totally gay down in Chelsea or Hell's Kitchen, but he was hoping to stick closer to home. Greg acquiesced even though Milton did not. Making plans with a friend made Preston think of Alanna and he knew he owed her a call or text, especially to update her about his sleepover with Todd.

Greg arrived with his boyfriend Marcus shortly after Preston had walked into the crowded bar area off 85th

Street. Marcus was a dapper-looking African American interior designer with an immaculately trimmed goatee and multiple gold studs pierced into both ears. He had a low, smooth voice and a calm demeanor that perfectly offset Greg's hyper, flamboyant side. It was a lovely May evening, so patrons were clamoring for space in the outdoor shed area that had been erected during the Covid pandemic and was now a fixture of the establishment. Just as Preston had finished hugging his friends in greeting, a small party of very young guys got off their bar stools to move outside. The three of them pounced on the available seats.

Squirming on his barstool, Greg cooed, "Oooh, it's still warm."

"Settle down, Daddy," Marcus teased.

They ordered cocktails, and Greg immediately asked Preston, "So why were you holed up inside all day in this gorgeous weather?"

Preston didn't want to admit to his newfound Titanic obsession so instead he replied, "I had a big date last night, and then I had to self-tape an audition for *The Equalizer*."

"Oh, I love that show," Marcus enthused. "Queen Latifah is a goddess."

"Wait a minute," Greg interrupted. "A date so big that you couldn't leave the house the next day? Define 'big' and spill it, Press."

"Nothing to spill," he told them with a nonchalant air and taking a sip of his margarita, careful to avoid the green paper umbrella adorning the glass. "A very nice guy. We went to The Waverly then came home and fooled around."

"No, no. I've known you too long not to realize when you're dancing around the real story."

Preston couldn't face the eye-rolling ridicule, even if it was good-natured, he'd face if he owned up to what had really been going on. Still, he managed to be honest by explaining, "He's a nurse practitioner. Super sweet and good looking. Maybe just not enough edge for me."

"Vanilla," Marcus said, nodding knowingly. "No one's favorite flavor."

"Press, you have a habit of favoring guys you know you can't have. You sabotage yourself every time," Greg observed without finesse.

That was probably true, Preston admitted to himself but defended with, "Why commit to one Mr. Right when you can have…"

"Mr. Right Now," they finished in unison.

First Alanna and now Greg? Preston adored them, but he wasn't about to let them head-shrink him.

Greg continued, "We're not kids anymore."

"I didn't realize I was having happy hour with my mother. Cheers, Mom," Preston raised his glass before downing the rest of his drink. He then signaled to the bartender for another round.

"The aimless actor's life. Unless you get a Broadway show or a TV series, there's no stability. We need to find you someone you can rely on."

"My sweet best friend, Greg. You have found me rental properties in the Hamptons, the perfect cashmere turtlenecks at Ralph Lauren, and the right pills when I need to drop weight quickly. But you can't find me a relationship when I'm not looking for one."

Greg gratefully received his next beverage and challenged his friend by asking, "If you're not looking for one, why did you go on a movie date with the nurse? Did the Waverly suddenly start showing gay porn?"

Preston looked at Marcus with a smirk and asked, "When did your boyfriend, the investment banker, get his degree in psychology?"

Greg was on a roll. "Maybe you're subconsciously trying to broaden your horizons by liking a different kind of guy. That doesn't make you schizophrenic."

Marcus suggested, "We could do a double date with the nurse sometime. Give him a chance to come out of his shell."

Preston was growing rapidly irritated and eager to change the subject. He resisted the urge to bark back at them, knowing he'd immediately regret it as he had with Alanna and then have to spend a fortune making it up to them with cocktails.

He finally managed to change the subject by asking Marcus about his latest design project in a downtown restaurant owned by a celebrity chef. There was no further mention of Todd, and the men finished up their drinks, bantering about Taylor Swift's love life and the current state of the *Real Housewives* of Somewhere.

The weather was so pleasant that Preston walked them down Broadway to the 79th Street subway station where they parted ways. He realized he was only a block away from Bon Soir and stopping in there for a little anonymous titillation might be just what he needed to blow off steam. He would be sure to keep an eye out for the asshole with the big dick and open jeans.

As he approached the green door, Milton summoned the will to stop him before he could ring the intercom for entry. Preston didn't understand. He wasn't intentionally hesitating. He wanted to go inside, so why was he stopping in his tracks? Some people walked by, and he wondered if he looked strange to them, like a zombie in the middle of the sidewalk? Then again, this was New York City. There were zombies everywhere.

Milton wanted him to go home and read a book. Call Todd. Or go to bed.

Preston couldn't seem to move forward to the door. He could only walk away, and he slowly started up Broadway in a daze that hadn't been caused by the margaritas. Maybe Greg and Marcus had hit a nerve, he fleetingly thought.

A block away was a longtime fixture in the neighborhood, the Westsider Rare and Used Books store, a tiny and crowded closet of an establishment with an ancient, narrow staircase leading to a small second-floor loft space. Every inch of the place was packed with volumes of books ranging from pristine art books and historical volumes, to beat up mathematics textbooks, and yellowed, paperback potboilers. There was always a cart stacked with piles by the front door, placed there to lure potential customers inside.

Milton made him stop to peruse among them, wondering if *Ethan Frome* might be buried in there somewhere. He had never had the chance to find out how it ended.

A musty softcover book with a very 1970s-looking couple embracing on a beach caught his eye. The man and woman smiling as they gazed into each other's eyes reminded Preston of pictures he'd seen of his parents in that era. *You Were Born Again to Be Together* by Dick Sutphen, according to the cover, claimed "The one you love today you have loved before in another life. Documented cases of reincarnation that prove love is immortal."

Preston began to thumb through it, reading along with Milton, a few pages espousing the concept that intimate relationships in your life are directly related to ones from a past life—or, in some cases, multiple previous lives. He'd never thought metaphysically but found it interesting, nonetheless.

Buy this book, Milton said to him in a voice Preston could actually hear. It sounded so much like his own that he assumed he was thinking out loud.

He fished a five dollar bill out of his wallet and stepped inside the cramped store to make the purchase.

A half hour later, Preston was sprawled on his sofa reading through the book and its accounts of "regressions."

It seemed to Preston like some sort of psychobabble that would probably make for a good reality show hosted by Dr. Phil or even David Copperfield. For Milton, however, it seemed to make sense. He may not have been "born again" but he certainly could see glimpses of Jack Thayer in Todd the nurse practitioner. Or was it imaginative, wishful thinking? If the book's premise was even remotely true, Jack was out there somewhere, whether or not they were ever destined to reunite.

Preston scoffed at the idea of "soul mates," yet continued reading until he dozed off in his living room, much to Milton's frustration. He wanted to continue, but as hard as he tried, he couldn't get Preston to stir. There was something reassuring in the stories of emotions so strong that they could transcend time and physicality. At least Milton did manage to conjure the banister memory after he'd farewelled Jack, which, of course for Preston, was only a dream.

It provided just enough stimulus to rouse Preston off the sofa and into the bedroom, where he slept soundly until nine o'clock the next morning, without ever flipping on the white noise machine. He woke to texts from Alanna checking in, and his mother asking him if he planned to come home for a visit anytime soon, otherwise she and his father would like to arrange a trip to see him in New York City. There was also an email from his agent notifying him of an audition in two days for an Off-Broadway musical.

The musical was the popular and irreverent parody of James Cameron's film, *Titanic*. Entitled *Titanique*, it was a silly send-up, featuring the characters from the movie (including the iceberg!), all set to a jukebox score of pop icon Celine Dion's songs. A Dion impersonator is the narrator of the story, and, as crazy a concept as it was, the show had developed a cult following and had been enjoying multiple extended runs since its premiere two years earlier. Preston was realizing there was no end to the public's thirst for all-things Titanic.

The audition criteria detailed in his agent's email called for him to "prepare 32 bars of an audition song in the style of, but not from, the show. Bring a copy of your resume, a recent headshot, and sheet music in an appropriate key. An accompanist will be provided. No a cappella, please." He would be considered for the roles of Jack Dawson and Cal Hockley, portrayed in the movie by Leonardo DiCaprio and Billy Zane, respectively. Preston was sure he'd have a better shot at playing the oily, villainous Cal over the fair-haired young hero.

He was probably one of the few gays in New York who hadn't seen the play, so he texted Greg to ask his advice on what to sing. Meanwhile, rather than flipping on the morning news, he began to stream a podcast episode, which featured *Titanique*'s director and co-creator, Tye Blue, as the guest. He might as well do a little research while having coffee.

It seemed like the show was a camp-fest but still a loving tribute to the 1997 film. Preston certainly appreciated that sort of humor and could quote lines from *Legally Blonde* or dance the "Time Warp" from *Rocky Horror*, with the best of them, but he felt uneasy about mocking a real-life tragedy that took such a terrible toll on human lives. Was a 9-11 themed drag show next?

His phone pinged to alert that Greg had replied to his text. It read, "Definitely ABBA."

"Dancing Queen" was part of Preston's karaoke repertoire, and he actually had the sheet music. He dug through his filing cabinet to find it and selected the 32-bar portion he would sing for the audition. It was a far cry from his original, loftier career goals of doing Ibsen or Shakespeare on Broadway. It was with those intentions in mind that he'd convinced his skeptical parents to let him skip college and head directly to the American Academy of

Dramatic Arts, straight out of high school (where he ultimately learned more about fellatio and bondage than he did about Chekhov or Tennessee Williams). But a job was a job.

Greg's texts weren't the only ones coming in. Todd was trying valiantly to reach out in a casual way with regular "How's it going" and "Just checking in" messages which Preston couldn't bring himself to answer. He hated ghosting such a nice guy, but he didn't want to pointlessly lead him on, either.

On the morning of the audition, Preston selected a darker, more conservative suit than he would have ordinarily worn. Unaware that it had been Milton's influence, Preston didn't give it a second thought when he passed by his standard navy blazer, light blue button-down shirt, and chinos. He scrutinized his appearance in the full-length mirror on the back of his bathroom door and decided he needed a haircut but otherwise liked how he looked. He should dress up more often, he decided.

As it was an unseasonably warm day, he treated himself to an Uber to avoid arriving at the Union Square theater as sweaty as he would get on the subway. He would be finished by noon and, since he was wearing a suit, invited Alanna to meet him for lunch at the nearby upscale Industry

Kitchen, downtown. Along with his headshot, resume and music, he tossed the paperback book into his grey Lululemon crossbody bag, a must-have for any aspiring actor "making the rounds." He'd finished reading the book the night before and thought Alanna might enjoy it.

Nestled at a corner table in the stunning eatery overlooking the East River, Preston held his head in his hands and had yet to so much as touch the beautiful fattoush salad the waiter had placed before him.

"I choked, Alanna. I completely choked."

"I'm sure you're exaggerating and were fine," she consoled, adding some sweetener to her iced tea.

"No, it was a disaster. Not only did my voice crack, I went up on the lyrics. I mean, how could I blow the words to Dancing Queen!? How many thousands of times have I sung that song?"

"I've heard you do it at least thirty times."

He looked up at her, wide eyed. "Exactly! The pianist very nicely suggested we try it a second time, but by then I was shattered."

Milton felt terribly guilty about it. He had never been on stage let alone the center of attention to anyone besides his adoring parents, and the sensation was almost as terrifying as that last night on Titanic.

"I haven't felt like myself in weeks. I haven't been screwing around or doing any drugs. I haven't even had a hangover," Preston admitted.

"Sweetie," she began delicately, "After our last conversation, I hesitate to get into this…"

"Just say it," he interrupted with an air of futility. He was starting to get used to being sermonized.

"I don't want to slut-shame you, but you have been very 'popular' as long as I've known you. Unapologetically. I know you well enough to put it to you this way, I think you're evolving."

"I appreciate your diplomacy, but I don't think I like where this is going."

"It's not like you're putting on weight or losing your hair, but…" she continued.

"But you're saying it's an age thing?"

"I'm saying it's a maturity thing. Press, you're growing up."

He'd heard the reprimands and guilt trips from his parents and rolled his eyes or shrugged it off. When Greg said it, it was jokey. From Alanna, though, it hit home.

A bus boy came by the table to refill their water glasses, and they paused their conversation. Preston was grateful for the distraction and managed to admire the fellow's perky backside as he turned away.

"Maybe you want something more substantial out of life than random quickies. I haven't found anyone I'd ever want to marry, but that doesn't mean I don't believe in the possibility."

That reminded him of the book, and he stopped her to fish through his bag for the copy he'd brought her. He produced it and was excited to hand it to her.

She looked at the title and said it aloud, "You Were Born Again to Be Together."

"Not just lovers, but it goes into how all the important relationships in your life could be holdovers or continuations from ones in previous lives. Even our enemies or rivals."

"That explains a lot about my father," she dryly quipped. "This book looks older than I am. Where'd you find it?"

"At a used bookstore on Broadway. Something told me to buy it."

"Something? Or someone? Maybe your past life is catching up with you, Pres.," she suggested with good humor. "Or you have a guardian angel. It is a miracle you don't get into more trouble."

Milton came to attention when she said this, wondering if that explained how he'd ended up there. To protect Preston from himself.

"Ever since we watched *The Poseidon Adventure* and I saw the Queen Mary, I've been thinking about it more and more. And then, all of a sudden, the Titanic keeps popping up everywhere. Like the audition today. I'm starting to believe there's a connection."

"There is a reason for everything, I believe," she observed before taking a bite of her chicken Caesar salad. "Even coincidences. Some might say, especially coincidences."

Lowering his voice conspiratorially, he proposed, "Do you think it's possible? Could I have been a passenger on the Titanic? In a past life?"

"Of course, you would have to die in the most famous shipwreck of all time. No obscure, random accident is good enough for you, babe," she teased.

"Okay, okay," he said, trying to be a good sport.

"Maybe before that you were King Tut. Or Cleopatra!"

"Enough!" he told her at full voice. "This is exactly why I didn't want to bring it up. I don't need to be mocked. And I'm not a child."

Alanna put down her fork and tried to reassure her friend. "Press, I've made a zillion errors in judgement. Betty Ford got rich from cases like me. It's why I try never to judge other people. Especially ones I love." She reached across the table and placed her hand on his, lovingly, almost maternally, "You don't need to go to a regressionist to find out if you had a past life. If you believe it, then it's real."

My sweet, supportive friend, he thought to himself, biting his tongue and convinced she'd lived through way too much psychobabble during her many years of therapy.

Listen to her, Milton told Preston, firmly.

Chapter Five

Milton embraced the notion of watching over Preston. Having lived his life as a gentleman of leisure, he had been unaccustomed to much personal responsibility other than maintaining the propriety of upper-class societal norms. In this world, however, there seemed to be few boundaries, and that was quite obviously not always for the better.

The streets of New York City had always included the poor, the homeless, and the disabled among its citizenry, but an atmosphere of lawlessness seemed to be pervasive now, in spite of all the wealth and opportunity that surrounded it. Even the smallest items in drug stores were locked behind protective barriers, uncouth and unsanitary conditions spilled out along the sidewalks, and rude behavior permeated even the most elegant neighborhoods. If chivalry wasn't dead, Milton thought, it was certainly gravely ill.

Even during his scholarly pursuits and while traveling around the great modern cities of Europe, Milton had never seen such blatant sexuality as was rampant everywhere he now looked. Whatever had happened to the civilized world between the sinking of Titanic and where he found himself now had been seismic. In his memory, homosexual acts had been criminalized or severely legislated in most places, codes of conduct were rigidly self-enforced by most, and lascivious behavior, while certainly existent, was neither discussed nor encouraged. Otherwise, Archibald Butt and Frances Millet would have been completely ostracized from the genteel society in which they thrived.

All he could do was try to navigate Preston away from danger and self-destruction, which seemed accessible everywhere. Whether it was the temptations of harmful substances or illicit sex, the dangerous distractions of ear buds on a busy street full of speeding cars and E-bikes traveling in the wrong direction, or the precarious ledge between the subway platform and the tracks, there were hazards everywhere. Thanks to Milton, Preston now had "eyes in the back of his head" and unwittingly moved about the City with not just increased caution but additional confidence as well.

One thing Milton held no sway over was getting Preston to return Todd's text messages. He'd like to have seen the good-looking nurse practitioner again, but Preston's resistance was too strong. Todd eventually gave up on trying to connect.

In spite of her concern for his social behavior, Alanna's support for Preston's conjecture of having been aboard Titanic gradually began to bolster him. Her words, "If you believe it, then it's real," stuck in his head as he went about his daily life and spent much of his free time reading up on various maritime disasters. In addition to Titanic, he was intrigued by and interested in the sad stories of the Lusitania, Andrea Doria, and Morro Castle.

As for his best friend, Preston decided his newfound mystical musings would be best kept unmentioned for now, lest he endure catty criticisms and commentary. Greg, meanwhile, had ordered Preston in no uncertain terms not to make any plans for his milestone birthday without consulting him first, and that he intended to put a deposit on an event venue.

"If you back out," Greg warned, "I'll have my own damned party."

It was remarkable to Milton the difference between being twenty-nine years of age in 1912 versus 2024. Not only had times changed, but people had. Where he had been considered somewhat of an oddity for being single and childless, Preston and his generation of peers were comparatively carefree and unfettered by those kinds of expectations. Milton was still weighing whether or not that was a change for the better, particularly when he observed openly affectionate same sex couples. Didn't they appreciate the privilege and freedom they were enjoying, expressing themselves in such a manner? Why would they treat intimacy so casually when they could strive to have the kind of deep, lasting commitment as his own parents or the Strauses?

During New York's annual Fleet Week celebrations at the end of May, Preston and Milton were drawn to all the Navy ships, Coast Guard vessels, and Naval Academy Patrol boats that arrived for the celebration. Ship tours were available, and Preston took several in hopes of experiencing some flash of recognition while on board. Nothing materialized for him spiritually, but having 2,300 strapping young service members in town eager to interact with an admiring public was certainly a plus.

Over the course of the week, Preston engaged a few sailors and marines in polite conversation but, while not averse to a casual sexual encounter, he didn't really find any of them particularly attractive…no matter how well some filled out their dress whites. Preston may have been more observant of their back sides, but Milton searched their faces in vain hopes of finding a glimmer of Jack among them. There was nothing.

On a temperate, gray afternoon in early June, Preston found himself sitting on a canvas folding chair outside the Pier i Cafe, which was on the Hudson Riverfront at West 70th Street. He was one of a half-dozen attractive young people hired to appear in a commercial for NYC tourism. The entire ad would feature different enticing scenarios around the city, all with the tagline "What's Good in N.Y.C.?"

As was usually the case with film shoots, most of the actors' time was spent waiting around. The director was holding out for a break in the clouds to take advantage of some sunshine, at which point the assembled cast and crew would be expected to jump to attention and simulate a rollicking outdoor celebration. Preston's role was to sit at a festively festooned cafe table with the actress portraying his girlfriend, toasting their glasses of wine as she looked into the camera to recite the scripted tagline.

While they waited and watched the skies, Preston was engrossed in the latest vintage book he'd purchased on Amazon, a well-preserved paperback edition of 1979's *The Titanic: End of a Dream* by author Wyn Craig Wade. Much of it focused on the Senate subcommittee hearings that occurred in the wake of the disaster, with heart-wrenching, emotional testimony from many of the surviving passengers and crew, including White Star's own J. Bruce Ismay, Colonel Archibald Gracie, Quartermaster Robert Hichens, Lookout Frederick Fleet, Junior Marconi Operator Harold Bride, and the captain of the rescue ship Carpathia, Arthur Rostron.

The weathered dust jacket touted "Here for the first time is the story of America's involvement in the Titanic disaster," and the author included an interesting, controversial take on "Anglo-American" failure as contributing to the social injustices condoned by the "Age of Security and Splendor." The statistics for the survival rate between classes were well documented and unfortunate.

His First-Class ticket should have increased Milton's odds for survival. Sixty-two percent made it home compared to forty-one percent of second-class and a mere twenty-five percent of steerage. The disproportionate devastation was well covered by the press of the day, but there had been no such privilege of escape for Milton. Nor had Jack's wealth afforded him a place in a lifeboat.

Preston felt like he could identify. Thanks to all the advantages he took for granted as the well-to-do only child from an affluent, Anglo-Saxon, white-collar suburb, he'd never really had to suffer or struggle for much besides paying for new headshots or rallying back from a horrendous hangover. If an anxiety attack could send him into a tailspin, how would he have handled being confronted with a colossal disaster at sea? Would he have had the pluck or luck to survive?

One passage in particular piqued Preston's interest and brought Milton to attention. In describing the final moments of Titanic before she disappeared beneath the surface, the author recounted the fate of young Philadelphian railroad heir John "Jack" Thayer and an unnamed friend who managed to stay on the ship until its very final moments. As described, Jack was able to survive by leaping from the ship and clinging to the keel of a collapsible lifeboat in the freezing Atlantic. His friend, holding on to the railing, was sucked under the black waters.

The tale intrigued Preston because he thought immediately of the similar imagery of his banister-sliding dream. For Milton, it meant unimaginable, unexpected joy to know that Jack had survived. Revelations for them both.

Simultaneously finishing the chapter, the clouds overhead parted, and the entire pier was suddenly bathed in bright afternoon sunlight. Almost instantly, the floor manager's voice boomed over a loudspeaker, "Places everybody, places. Reposition cameras."

As soon as Preston got home, he changed into a comfortable tank top and a pair of yoga pants, then hit the sofa with his laptop and googled the words "Jack Thayer Titanic." The search results were extensive, and Preston was immediately drawn to the first photograph he saw displayed. He clicked on images, and Milton gasped so loudly that Preston vocalized it himself.

There were scores of photos, many of them duplicates, of the handsome young man with the sensual mouth and prominent ears. In some, he was a student in his cricket gear. In others he wore a suit, as Milton had seen him.

"Sexy," Preston murmured, approvingly. "Glad you survived, baby boy."

Along with the photographs were images of six drawings made aboard the Carpathia the day after the disaster, according to Jack's testimony. It documented for history how he claimed to have witnessed Titanic break apart, even though many eyewitnesses claimed it slid to its fate in one piece, as depicted in the early movie versions. Of course, when oceanographer Robert Ballad discovered the wreck in 1985, using Jack's detailed and accurate account to help him pinpoint the precise location, he was proven right.

Jack ended up a hero in the autopsy of the disaster in its immediate aftermath as well as decades later.

Reading on, Preston learned that the split meant there would be a significant debris field between the bow and stern sections, comprised of the ship's contents. Consequently, that narrowed Ballard's search, and those relics would ultimately lead him to the wreck discovery that astounded the world and reignited Titanic-mania for further generations to come.

Milton felt pride and, consequently, so did Preston who examined the sketches with keen interest.

First, the majestic ship strikes the giant iceberg before settling by the head and the forward stack breaking at one-forty in the morning. "Forward end floats then sinks," he expertly described with focused detail. He showed the stern section on its own at two oh-eight and then finally standing perpendicular and in "last position in which Titanic stayed for 5 minutes before the final plunge."

Preston continued to scan the abundant results hungrily.

According to a privately published account in 1940, Jack was quoted as saying that prior to that terrible night, "There was peace, and the world had an even tenor to its way. It seems to me that the disaster about to occur was the event that not only made the world rub its eyes and awake, but woke it with a start, keeping it moving at a rapidly accelerating pace ever since, with less and less peace, satisfaction, and happiness. To my mind the world of today awoke April 15, 1912."

Upon reading this, Milton felt himself gasp again, and this time it literally took Preston's breath away. Jack had perfectly expressed in his testimony how Milton was feeling in this changed universe of 2024. And it was the sinking of Titanic that had sparked the evolution.

Preston was about to click on another image, but Milton wasn't finished reading and forced him to continue with the article on the browser.

Jack recollected more of his view from the water. "Groups of the fifteen hundred people still aboard, clinging in clusters of bunches like swarming bees; only to fall in masses, pairs, or singly as the great afterpart of the ship— two hundred fifty feet of it—rose into the sky." Swimmers flailing in the icy sea sounded "like the high-pitched hum of locusts on a midsummer night in the woods back home in Pennsylvania" before quickly fading to silence. The fact that the half-filled lifeboats did not return to rescue those still stranded and freezing to death in the water justifiably haunted all the survivors.

Preston googled where in Pennsylvania the Thayer's had lived. It was the Philadelphia suburb of Haverford, not far from where he himself had grown up in West Chester.

Another account named his friend. Milton Long.

Milton felt a thrill at being named and remembered by Jack. For Preston, this elicited not only a snicker but a revelation. He suspected just what kind of "friend" this pretty boy had made.

Preston's mental wheels turned rapidly. People have been mistakenly calling me 'Milton' my entire life, he said to himself. It may not have been accidental, at all.

"Milton Long and I had been standing by the rail, about abreast of the second funnel. Our main thought was to keep away from the crowd and the suction. At the rail we were free of the crowd. We had no time to think now, only to act. He climbed over the rail, sliding down facing the ship, only 12 or 15 feet above the water."

Preston and Milton shivered.

"I never saw Long again. His body was later recovered. I am afraid that the few seconds elapsing between our going meant the difference between being sucked down into the deck below, as I believe he was, or pushed out by the backwash."

They remembered sliding down but nothing further.

There were a few more images of Jack later in life, still attractive even with those ears. His toothy, winning smile, however, never reappeared.

※ ※ ※

For Milton, it was that seemingly indelible smile that made Jack even more attractive than his unblemished complexion and thick, glossy hair. He had been wearing it every time Milton noticed him onboard the ship, gleaming white and as eye-catching as a sparkler. Prior to their actual meeting on Titanic's final night, Milton had spotted him in the dining room and on the Promenade deck with his parents, but the very first glimpse of him now returned to his mind's eye.

His steward, William, had just finished unpacking his wardrobe when Milton decided to have a stroll around the magnificent vessel and get his bearings for the week ahead at sea. He decided to walk up the Grand Staircase to C-Deck, where he could purchase some postcards in the purser's office and then take them to one of the public rooms and enjoy a beverage while he wrote a note to his parents. He had been remiss in doing so since he had departed

Marseilles to meet the ship in Southampton. Better yet, perhaps he could find a cozy corner in the Reception Room, decorated in the Jacobean style, with beautiful windows and a grand piano.

At the staircase, he instantly recognized John Jacob and Madeleine Astor, on their way back to the upper decks after getting their beloved Airedale, Kitty, settled in the ship's kennel. Milton held back a moment, long enough to allow them to go ahead of him.

No sooner had he placed his hand on the solid Irish oak banister of the staircase to begin his ascent than he noticed Jack stepping lively downwards from his private stateroom. Like Milton, he was unaccompanied, but smiling nonetheless. There was an unmistakable joie de vivre in his expression that went beyond just the usual excitement of setting sail on a transatlantic journey. This, Milton immediately thought, was not only a good-looking person; he was a happy person. It was a marvelous trait for a first impression, and Milton speculated how he, himself, was perceived by others. If they even really noticed him at all.

※ ※ ※

Jack Thayer would live to the age of fifty but did not have a happy ending from what they read online. Although he went on to marry a woman named Lois Cassatt and have five children, one of whom perished in World War II, Jack would never recover from the trauma of Titanic. His father had perished during the sinking, but his beloved mother, whom Milton could so vividly remember laughing gaily with her lovely son, lived until the 32nd anniversary of the catastrophe and then died suddenly.

Already suffering from depression and what would today be diagnosed as post-traumatic stress, Jack could bear no more loss after three decades without peace. He drove himself from the stately family home, parked his car, and proceeded to slash his wrists and throat. Forty hours passed before his body was discovered.

Preston, unaware his eyes had filled with tears, wasn't prepared to be so moved. Milton wasn't prepared for the disclosure. They felt a simultaneous head rush that was not unlike a poppers high, just as short and intense. But as soon as it subsided, their conjoined emotions intangibly changed whatever was happening between them. Preston tried to shake it off and continue reading, but Milton was no longer in and out of the background. He was right there with Preston; two minds, one body.

Even after Titanic, Preston read, Jack had managed to go on to live the life that was expected of him by marrying, becoming a father and serving a distinguished career in finance with his alma mater, the University of Pennsylvania. Along with all the other "what ifs" that went along with the story of the ill-fated ship, Milton tried not to dare imagine what if they had both arrived in New York City as they had planned before the collision with the iceberg.

Preston clicked back to the image of smiling Jack and enlarged it. He then printed out the photograph and placed it on his kitchen counter. Was he only imagining that he bore a resemblance to Todd, the nurse?

The next day, Preston decided to forgo a lunch date with Alanna in favor of hitting the gym, and he did so with the added vigor of having Jack Thayer in the front of his mind. Jack was rich and handsome…and had survived one of the greatest maritime disasters of all time, only to ultimately succumb to its terrible legacy of hubris. The information was a wake-up call for Preston, who realized he should make the most of every precious moment. He hadn't heard from Alanna but reading Jack's biography had made a difference. He started by spending two hours on the treadmill, pumping iron and then in the sauna, forgoing any tempting quickies with all the willing towel-wearing hunks.

On his way out of the Equinox Fitness Club, he grabbed a healthy juice with added protein and chia seeds before stopping by the barber shop down the block from his apartment. He sat in the chair and had the cape drawn around him as the barber asked him how he wanted his hair cut. He reached for his phone and pulled up the photo of Jack, his thick dark hair cut short but longer on top, with a classic side part.

"Neaten it up. Like this."

Looking fresh with his new cut, Preston was pleased with the resulting effect. There was a Banana Republic in between the barber shop and his street, so he spontaneously decided to stop in there and pick up some clothes that would suit his new, more classic look.

He came home with three shopping bags filled with socks, khaki pants, as well as a half dozen fitted dress shirts, all in plain colors he would have always found boring. Less so, now. White, beige, light blue, taupe, tan, and a soft yellow. He unpacked and put them neatly into his closet before settling onto the sofa with his laptop. He intended to spend the afternoon doing a deep dive into whatever happened to Milton Long.

It wasn't difficult to find the basic information about his short life. He lived with his parents at 42 Pearl Street in Springfield, Massachusetts and stood at 5'10 with brown hair, grey-blue eyes and a thin face, according to his passport. An acquaintance described him as "a young man of delicate refinement and handsome to an unusual degree." Before he departed on his European travels, Milton had gifted his pocket watch to the family chauffeur. There was a photograph of it, accompanied by one of him, looking appropriately serious for the era in which he lived.

His body was recovered by the Mackay Bennett, a ship engaged by the White Star Line. He was found wearing his suit with a monogrammed shirt and handkerchief, brown boots, and personal effects that included a gold wristwatch, gold ring with crest, and three gold studs.

His remains were forwarded to his parents, and he was buried in the Springfield Cemetery. When his parents eventually passed away—his doting mother, having lived to age ninety-five—they were interred alongside him. Preston found an image of the impressive headstone that included the inscription "The seas are quiet, when the winds give o'er; so calm are we when passions are no more." He read and reread it, working to decipher its meaning.

Most notable to Preston was Milton's date of birth, October 19, 1882. They shared a birthday!

Preston clicked over to another page and discovered that the Longs had corresponded with Jack Thayer about his brief friendship with their son. Milton felt a rush of excitement as Preston scrolled down the page. Not only had Jack remembered him but had reached out to Mother and Dad!

Milton thought of how much that must have meant to his parents and how much it meant to him now. Along with Preston, he read Jack's recounting to them, "Your son was sitting in front and to one side of us at dinner that last evening. He looked lonely, and I was lonely. At the last part, he was perfectly calm all the time and kept his nerve even to the very end."

Lonely was the last word Milton would ever have thought to describe Jack Thayer. If it was so, he had expertly hidden it behind that winning smile and lively personality.

Jack was right about him, Milton knew. He had been lonely and lost. All the rambling years bouncing between universities and traveling by himself. Then, a single encounter later, he'd found himself on the precipice of purpose. He could never have imagined that someone as gregarious and magnificent as Jack could have been feeling alone, too.

Touchingly, Jack had sent a photograph of himself to Milton's parents, writing, "I am sending you my picture, thinking you might like to see who was with him at the end. I would treasure it very much if you could spare me one of his."

Preston wondered if he could ever feel that way about a man. Milton had been enormously attracted to and captivated by Jack Thayer, but after reading this, he knew that it was love. And it had been mutual.

The sun was already setting by the time Preston put down the laptop. He'd been sitting in the same position for so long that his legs were cramped, and he got up to stretch. Reading about the Long and Thayer families had made him think of his own parents and how remiss he had been about visiting them, even though they were only a two-hour train ride away.

He ordered some Chinese food and decided to call his folks while waiting for the delivery.

"Hi, Mom, it's me," he announced when Liz Spaulding's pleasantly comforting voice picked up after a single ring.

"Preston, sweetheart, this is a nice surprise."

That made him feel guilty, and he speculated if that had been her very intention for saying it.

He told his mother how much she would like his new haircut and the new wardrobe he had purchased. "Very preppy. Totally your style."

"I've always told you that's your best look, darling," she assured him.

After he went through the details of his spree, she jumped back in with, "Hold on, your dad wants to say hello." This was their telephone ritual, and he knew well the routine from almost every call since he'd moved away from home.

"Hello, son," Brandon Spaulding's deep voice greeted.

"What's happening, dad," he asked, ready for a report on golf games or politics.

But his father regaled him with news on the museums in Philadelphia they had been visiting lately, including a new gallery at The Barnes Foundation and a Titanic Exhibition at the Franklin Institute.

Preston seized on the mention and quickly jumped in to ask, "How was it? Will it be going on for a while?"

"It was very good. I think it's there all summer. I didn't know you had an interest. I seem to remember you barely passed history when you were in high school."

Ignoring the not-so subtle dig, Preston suggested, "I'd love to check it out next time I'm home."

"You know your mom and I would love that. When can you make it happen?"

"I was actually thinking about coming in for a weekend soon."

They compared calendars and came up with a date.

"You're coming home for a visit?" He heard his eavesdropping mother call out from the background. "Oh, goodie!"

After the call, Preston ate his stir-fried chicken and steamed vegetable dumplings while watching CNN. The printed image of Jack's photograph was still on the kitchen counter, and he found himself frequently glancing back at it. Did he seem familiar, or was he just reminded of Todd?

He stood up and looked into the mirror on the wall across from the kitchen. Scrutinizing his face, he looked for any resemblance to the single photo of Milton with his grey-blue eyes, thin face and aquiline nose. Should there be similarities, he asked himself. Even with the haircut, he didn't see it.

Milton looked at Preston's reflection in the mirror. He didn't miss his face; he was perfectly satisfied with this one. And the new hair style was definitely an improvement.

Preston went back to his dinner and noticed the time on the clock. It was shortly after eight.

"What am I doing?" he said aloud, suddenly frustrated that he was at home eating take-out and spent an entire day obsessing about long dead people from over another century. That was the exact opposite of living life to the fullest.

Within minutes, he was out the door and into the night, making sure to muss his hair when he passed by the mirror.

The next thing he knew, he was groggily squinting from the morning sun pouring through his bedroom window and blinding him awake. His head throbbed and his teeth felt like they were wearing little sweaters. He rolled over and scrunched his eyes tightly shut, trying to piece together whatever he had gotten up to when he left the apartment the night before.

He recalled hailing a taxi and heading down to Industry, the popular club in Hell's Kitchen on West 52nd Street. After a brief wait in line to get inside, he had two or three vodka sodas before meeting a juiced-up muscle guy that looked not unlike Dom on steroids. There was immediate chemistry between them, and they took turns buying shots, a bad mix with the vodka, and Preston was quickly intoxicated.

With every round, Milton winced. Less from the alcohol than from Preston's vulgar behavior. Just as he'd begun to feel as if he could exert some helpful influence over his host, Milton could only now look on as he continued on his self-destructive, callow path.

He had no memory of leaving Industry, but he did remember following the hulking hunk home and climbing several flights of stairs in a nearby walk-up apartment building before getting naked together. As he recollected all the tattoos on his lover's massive biceps, pectorals, and even buttocks, he noticed he could smell the leathery cologne now on his own skin. It made his already queasy stomach do a flip.

"Must unswallow," he groaned, forcing himself upright so he could make his way to the bathroom. There was a trail of his clothes leading from the front door to his bed, although he hadn't managed to remove his left sock. He had no memory of traveling or arriving home, but was relieved his phone was there, albeit on the floor and with the battery fully drained. He checked his wallet which was on the table next to his keys and thanked God he hadn't taken any of the "emergency" ecstasy tablets he'd stashed there.

Almost to the bathroom, he avoided catching the sight of his hungover, haggard self in the wall mirror, but, after regurgitating the toxins of the night before, he couldn't circumvent the large, mirrored medicine chest.

He didn't see himself in the glass. It was Milton Long, angrily looking back at him, his brows furrowed and jaw clenched. Preston thought he must still be drunk and hallucinating.

"You disgust me," Milton said aloud in a clipped Mid-Atlantic accent. "Haven't I taught you anything?"

Chapter Six

The image of Milton's countenance in the single photograph he had discovered was now prominently etched in Preston's mind. He seemed to catch a glimpse of it in window reflections and in the faces of random people moving along on subways and sidewalks. He was even doing double-takes at the gym, where Milton's sober gaze seemed to be watching him through the eyes of weightlifters and treadmill runners.

It wasn't something Preston could shake or suppress with alcohol or Xanax. The reprimand coming from the mirror must not have been his imagination, but he couldn't bring himself to attempt conjuring up a ghost from the medicine chest without being a complete lunatic.

He finally dared it while running a loop of Central Park on an overcast weekday morning. Ear buds in and listening to one of his favorite Ed Sheeran and Adele playlists, he figured he could attempt to reach out in the comparative isolation of the Park without looking like a crazy person. Not that there was any shortage of crazy persons in Central Park.

Starting to breathe hard as he curved around 110th Street where the scenic Meer was undergoing an extensive renovation, he charged up Harlem Hill and ventured "Milton? I want you to talk to me again. If you can. Milton?"

Nothing. He pushed up the steep incline and tried again. "Milton, come on, you asshole. Talk to me."

He reached the summit of the hill and blinked away a salty stream of perspiration that had rolled down into his eye from his forehead.

"Why me? Why now? What do you want from me, Milton?"

Suddenly the music stopped playing.

I'm not to be summoned like a kitchen maid.

It sounded as clear as a bell.

"If we're sharing a body, don't I have the right to talk to you? You just popped in to yell at me."

Preston was unsure if he was speaking aloud or just thinking the words. He considered that maybe his parents were right to have sent him to a psychiatrist when he was a kid, talking to himself. Was all this some kind of mental breakdown? He continued running along, slowing to more of a jog.

I don't know what the rules are, any better than you, Preston. It is what it is.

"I never gave a flying fuck about the Titanic before."

It's not about Titanic. It's...about love.

"I never gave a flying fuck about that, either."

People change.

It dawned on Preston that Alanna had suggested he was evolving.

"You have to help me figure this out, Milton."

I feel like there's something we're supposed to figure out. Together. But do you suppose we could do it with a bit more decorum?

Preston found himself laughing and asked, "How would someone from your world tell you to 'pull the stick out of your ass!?'"

The music came back on and, as Preston began to pick up speed descending the running path on his way northward, he called out, "Oh, come on. Can't you take a joke?"

They had been coexisting for several weeks, but Preston was now fully aware of Milton's presence, and they were increasingly able to communicate their thoughts to each other. There was no one he could possibly tell, aside from perhaps Alanna. Even that would be risky and, given her own history in rehab, he didn't want to chance her pressuring him into professional counseling. Besides, Milton didn't frighten or disturb him. He was more like a conscience he could actually see and hear.

And feel. It was Milton who framed the printed photo of Jack and positioned it in the center of the bedroom bookshelf. It was also Milton who was excited by the prospect of a trip to Pennsylvania, longing to again feel the comfort of a parent's love. Perhaps to even see where the Thayers had lived, remembering the kind invitation Jack had extended for him to come and stay for a visit.

Preston and Milton headed to Pennsylvania for a weekend with the Spauldings in their classic but comfortable Tudor-style home in West Chester, overlooking a scenic golf course. As much as Preston had always despised the unreliable rickety train trip required to travel to and from New York's Penn Station, by allowing Milton to see the view as they bumped through New Jersey and the lush suburbs of Philadelphia's Main Line, it was like experiencing it for the first time. Many of the rolling hills and historic properties visible from the Amtrak car looked not too unlike how they would have appeared during Milton's lifetime.

The train pulled into the Paoli station, miraculously on time, and Preston noticed his parents' black Jaguar sedan in the depot parking lot adjacent to the platform. Even with its understated elegance, it stood out from all the other vehicles—mainly minivans and pickup trucks.

Preston could see his own reflection in the train window as they slowed to a stop, and the conductor announced, "This is Paoli Station. Please exit from the front of the train for Paoli." He could also see a glimpse of Milton's reflection and thought to himself, "He's not bad looking. But he needs to smile, once in a while."

I know what you're thinking, Preston, Milton warned, not without humor.

Preston chuckled, realizing he had to get used to housing two souls in a single body and then replied to Milton non-verbally, *Then know this. Do not embarrass me in front of my mom and dad, or I'll find myself an exorcist to get rid of you.*

Brandon and Liz Spaulding emerged from their car as soon as they saw the train pull in to discharge riders and excitedly waved at Preston when they spotted him heading toward them. As they always had, his parents jointly embraced him in a big, happy bear hug. Milton reacted to the feeling of physical parental affection that sent a shiver through Preston's body. Milton's father, as close as they were, had never hugged him like that.

"Oh, honey," Liz gushed, "It's been too long. We're so happy you're home."

Milton dared to allow himself a moment to indulge in the fantasy that this was his own mother, Harriet (whom everyone called "Hattie"), welcoming him back to their Springfield home as she always had after one of his extended trips away. There was something eternal about a mother's love. and he imagined he could smell her faint, floral perfume, *Quelques Fleurs*.

After putting Preston's small carry-on suitcase into the trunk of the car, the Spauldings headed back to West Chester for a big steak dinner to welcome their son home. Brandon had three filet mignons marinating and waiting to be grilled, and Liz had made an enormous batch of his favorite German potato salad made with mustard instead of mayonnaise and had shucked plenty of ears of corn. Since the weather continued to be the perfect transition time of spring to summer, they planned to dine in the lovely screened-in porch overlooking the swimming pool and garage that had been long ago converted into a combination pool house and guest quarters.

Preston didn't come back to West Chester often, but he had to admit that it felt good to be back there. A similar sense of nostalgia occurred to Milton, too, even though he'd never been to that part of Pennsylvania before. The climate, the vegetation, and the landscape of the countryside as the Spauldings drove along Paoli Pike all seemed to have an aura of familiarity to the New England countryside he'd known all during his life.

The Spaulding home was a large but cozy country home that reflected the quaint and historic nature of the Chester County area. Milton found it warm and welcoming, not just because of its owners, but because of the energy within its very walls, first erected in the second decade of the twentieth century. The architecture, from the carved stone surrounding the living room fireplace to the large stately wooden staircase near the front door, was reminiscent of the Long's own house. When Preston set his luggage at the foot of the steps, he made a point of mentally telling Milton that this was not the long, straight banister that matched the Titanic railing. That had been from the farmhouse staircase where the family had lived until Preston was eleven years old.

Their hearty dinner was accompanied by an excellent red wine Brandon had selected from their small but well-stocked wine cellar. He and Liz caught their son up on family and neighborhood news, and he, in turn, tried to make his routine rounds of auditions and occasional entertainment jobs sound busier and more productive than he knew they actually were.

"Remember Reese and Mary Friedman?" Liz asked, savoring a bit of gossip. "You went to junior high school with their twin girls."

"Vaguely," he answered, even though he had no clue who they were.

"Both girls turned out to be doctors. And both practice at Paoli Memorial. One's a dermatologist, and one's a gynecologist. I don't remember which one is which."

"Be careful not to go to the wrong one and get Botox in the wrong place."

She had to think about it for a moment and then giggled at the naughty innuendo.

"All right, you two," Brandon scoffed.

Preston defended himself, "Dad, she set me up for that one."

"It makes you think. Never too late to go back to school," Brandon remarked, trying to slip it into the conversation casually, even though he'd said it so many times before.

As usual, Liz intervened on behalf of their son by saying, "We know you're only one audition away from your big break. It will happen, Press. You're too talented for it not to."

Parents never changed, Milton thought. How many similar discussions had he had with his own over the dinner table when he chose to leave Columbia? Then Harvard? His brief stint as a law clerk? And almost every time before and after one of his long pleasure trips abroad.

This suspicion was only reaffirmed when Liz asked Preston about his love life, topping off his wine glass. "Are you dating anyone nice? Even the gays can give their parents grandbabies."

One of Hattie's last letters to Milton before he sailed on Titanic was a not-so-subtle reminder for him to be open to meeting some eligible young ladies with whom he might want to start raising a family.

"Mom, I don't even have any plants. I'm not interested in taking care of kids." To diffuse the awkward subject with humor, he flexed one of his impressive biceps and said, "But I'm taking excellent care of myself."

It immediately disarmed his mother, but his father was less easily persuaded and continued with his more serious approach by asking, "So, why the sudden interest in the Franklin Institute? You don't have enough museums in New York City?"

"Brandon, I'm just grateful to have him home," Liz chided.

"You mentioned the Titanic exhibition. I recently auditioned for an Off-Broadway musical about Titanic, and it just kind of piqued my interest, that's all. I've been reading up on it."

"Somewhere in the library we have a copy of Walter Lord's book. And, of course, we've seen the Kate Winslet movie," his mother said.

"Didn't we just see a documentary on TV about the submersible that imploded, diving to the wreck?" Brandon asked his wife.

"The Titan," Preston clarified, knowledgeably speaking about the 2023 tragedy that took the lives of five people who were on an expedition to descend to Titanic's final resting place. "A horrible example of what's called adventure tourism. Even Dr. Ballard, who discovered the wreck back in the 80's, thinks it's hallowed ground and should be left alone."

Brandon was impressed with his son's thoughtfulness on the subject and pleased to see him exhibit a more serious side. He encouraged him by asking, "So how will you feel about seeing recovered artifacts?"

"What's been brought up is here now, so there's no going back. But with A.I. and all the digital technology available, the entire site and even the interiors can be recreated virtually. There's no need to risk more lives being lost on top of all those killed back in 1912."

Milton was impressed with Preston, too.

That night, in the bedroom of his adolescence, Preston slept soundly without benefit of a sleeping pill or white noise machine. How many thousands of nights he had laid there, worrying about the endless anxieties of puberty and what his future would hold. How many fantasies he'd had about intimacies with other young men; the endless dreams of fame and fortune as a celebrity; the ultimate happy ending of a life in somewhere like NYC or Hollywood, even indulging in the hope of finding blissful love with another handsome, successful, and devoted man. Somewhere along the line, that particular aspiration had been squelched.

Tonight, though, Preston did not dream. It was Milton whose imagination was in overdrive with both memories of his past life and aspirations for what might still lie ahead for his wandering and unfulfilled spirit. Had the Spauldings stirred a homesickness for worldly pleasures he hadn't acknowledged, he asked himself. His recollected senses detected the aroma of the strong coffee their maid had waiting for him every morning and the scent of his father's pipe emanating from his study. Most vivid of all, he could recall every all-too brief moment he spent with Jack experiencing such rushes of diverse emotion in such a short span of time. The titillation of first seeing and meeting him with the subsequent, immediate attraction, the hopefulness for a post-voyage reunion dashed by a shocking turn of events and the terror of impending death. Fate or God or metaphysics had returned him to the earthly world and partnered him with this young gay man who was suddenly and miraculously interested in helping him complete his woefully unfinished story.

※ ※ ※

Since it was founded in 1824, Philadelphia's Franklin Institute was not only one of the city's most popular attractions for both locals and tourists, but also a premiere science and research center named for America's first man of science and the site of the majestic Benjamin Franklin Memorial which depicts the founding father in a 20 foot, 30 ton marble statue by sculptor James Earle Fraser. Like almost every child in Pennsylvania, Preston had gone there on more than one school field trip and felt a familiarity when entering the dramatic museum rotunda.

The current Titanic exhibition on display was from the Cunard-White Star Line, featured rare and unique artifacts and items, ranging from a massive Lego model replica of the ship to recovered paper effects, china, and clothing. Liz had decided that "once was enough" to see it and offered to meet her husband and son afterwards for dinner at the popular nearby restaurant, Barclay Prime. Brandon had no urgent need to return, either, but was looking forward to some rare father-son time and enthusiastically purchased tickets for them online before they boarded the SEPTA local train into Center City.

Much of the experience was designed for Titanic fans whose primary knowledge of the ship came from the film adaptations of her story. They were handed paper tickets replicating vintage boarding passes in a waiting area replicating the White Star pier and a two-story high side of the ship. Preston commended his dad for arranging to take them on a mid-afternoon when most of the kids were already gone, and only a few straggling tourists remained.

They entered through a mock D-Deck Reception area. Milton instinctively searched for his cabin, D6. Piped-in *The Blue Danube* music led them to a full-scale recreation of the Grand Staircase.

Preston had worked on enough film and TV sets to be unimpressed and thought it was corny, but Milton chided by telling him, *No. It's quite accurate.* They slowly descended the steps, holding on to the banister which expertly duplicated the original made from Irish oak. The famed clock, flanked by allegorical figures of *Honour and Glory Crowning Time,* was less convincing but the bronze cherub on the newel post of the staircase base was just as Milton remembered it, holding an illuminated torch. Display cases housing artifacts were artistically placed on the edges of the display, and they stopped to look at an assortment of small perfume bottles, a hand mirror, and some other glassware.

From there they walked down a First-Class hallway leading to a mini version of Titanic's Verandah Palm Court and Cafe. Here was where the majority of recovered china, crockery, carafes, and silverware were positioned for viewing.

"Aren't they something?" his father commented as they studied the place settings. Milton could almost taste his last meal of salmon hollandaise, and Preston could, too. He asked Brandon for a breath mint, knowing he always kept some in his pocket.

From there, they came to a corner of the Smoking Room as it would have appeared aboard Titanic and there were housed a man's monogrammed pocket watch, a silver cigarette case, an ashtray, some playing cards, and a half dozen books in remarkably well-preserved condition. Neither *Peter Pan* nor *Ethan Frome* was among them. Milton remembered the matchbooks he had collected, and, even though he was still sucking on a mint, Preston had a sudden, inexplicable urge for a cigarette. He had never smoked.

A First-Class cabin decorated in the Modern Dutch style looked nothing like the stateroom Milton occupied but may very well have been what some other passengers would have recognized. The Thayers had occupied two adjoining rooms on C-Deck with access to a private bathroom and a walk-in wardrobe. The display cases here showed off a man's comb and cufflinks, a lady's purse, and some shoes that had obviously belonged to a child.

Definitely from a steerage youngster, Milton recognized by their working class design, silently chastising whoever had placed them incorrectly in a First-Class setting. He remembered his own brown lace-up leather boots, which he had vowed to replace with more popular Oxfords, after having seen the trend proliferate while in Europe.

They lingered in an adjacent hall that housed an impressive assortment of larger, heavy recoveries. There was a telegraph, a safe door and a First-Class sink. It was all very well presented and interesting, Preston and Milton agreed, but nothing generated any personal flash of recognition they had expected from the visit. Not yet.

The final room of the exhibition was the most simply designed, but by far the most striking. At the entry, placed on a faceless mannequin inside an air-tight glass case, there was one of the only twelve known existing Titanic life jackets of the 3,000 that were on board. Made of hard cork and canvas, according to the exhibit label, these would prove worthy for flotation but dangerous for anyone jumping off the ship. Many passengers who leapt from the sinking vessel broke their jaws or were knocked out when striking the water, with the hard cork smashing into their heads. Another horrific aspect of an already unimaginable nightmare.

Milton felt reassured that hadn't happened to Jack, since he survived the ordeal.

They entered a dark room with a solitary blue light shining on an actual Titanic davit, one of the small cranes used to suspend and lower lifeboats, forever locked into its final position, and the curators had connected it to one of the James Cameron lifeboat replicas from his motion picture.

"Breathtaking," Brandon said quietly, not noticing that his son was beginning to tremble. He read aloud from the small placard mounted by the display. "Place your hand on the crank and imagine what it felt like to touch this as you attempted to board a lifeboat from the ever-listing ship."

Brandon felt it for himself, noticing the immovable mechanism as Preston shuddered, almost paralyzed in place.

Preston, touch it, Milton urged.

Milton's host could not lift up his hand, so he repeated to him, *Please, put your hand on it.*

Summoning as much physical strength and mental resolve as he could muster, Preston took a step closer and reached his hand out toward the davit's arm and base, made of large iron castings with milled steel and brass fittings. His pulse was pounding, and perspiration appeared on his forehead, in spite of the cool temperature at which the museum hall was kept. It was then that Brandon noticed Preston's tremulous movement and became concerned.

"Press, you okay?"

Milton kept pushing him to continue reaching for the metal until his fingers made contact with its surface. Preston appeared to be frozen in the position, but internally he felt a surge that felt like electricity tearing through his entire body.

This was it. This was the davit Milton had rested his hand upon when he and Jack had futilely asked to board a lifeboat more than 112 years before.

The voltaic charge felt as if it were fully fusing Preston and Milton, giving him equal possession of the solitary body they were sharing. They felt Brandon grab him by the upper arm.

"Son, what is it?"

Preston couldn't speak even after being jolted out of the moment. It was Milton who looked into Brandon's concerned face and breathlessly answered, "I'm fine. Let's get going."

They stepped away from the lifeboat display and made their way to the final passageway leading to the exhibition's exit. Plaintive Celtic flute music played as they moved through the corridor which had hundreds of vintage photographs reproduced with "Survived" on one side and "Perished" on the other.

Milton made them stop to examine the photographs, first on the "Survived" wall. It was easy to spot young, handsome Jack Thayer. It was the same picture he framed in his bedroom in New York.

"That's Jack Thayer."

"I remember the Thayers," Brandon told him. "I didn't know any of them personally, but everybody in my day had heard of them because of the Titanic, of course. Didn't Jack and his mother both survive?"

"Yes, but not his father."

Marian Thayer's picture was mounted beside her son's, her wistful gaze peering into the camera from another era. Surprisingly, at least as Milton remembered her, she had not even a hint of a smile. It must have been taken after the disaster.

Preston moved to the "Perished" display which was significantly larger and found John Borland Thayer easily as the images were arranged alphabetically.

Pointing to it, Milton said, *There.*

Taking a few steps further, moving his way up the alphabet to the L's, there was the only known image of Milton Clyde Long.

"And here I am."

A long, pregnant pause followed. Brandon, after his son's strange and emotional outburst in the exhibition, didn't have any response other than to ask, "What do you mean, 'here' you are?"

Preston found his voice and was able to answer for himself.

"Dad, Milton died on Titanic. But he's alive in me."

Chapter Seven

Liz Spaulding had secured the best table for them at Barclay Prime, a four-top in the center of the large, upscale dining room. However, when Brandon arrived with Preston and the maître d' was showing them to where she was already waiting, he discreetly passed the employee a twenty-dollar bill and requested a more private table somewhere in the back or in a corner.

As they were being led to the new seating, Liz followed. She was confused and concerned. Her husband looked agitated, and her son was sullen and silent. Milton had compelled Preston to grab a few of the restaurant's matchbooks when they entered, and he was engrossed in examining the cardboard folding cover and coarse exterior striking surface. Old habits die hard.

"What's going on? Did something happen?"

"You son's overactive imagination, again," Brandon answered quietly, between clenched teeth. "There were never any of these theatrics on my side of the family. Ever since you put him in that damned Peter Pan play as a kid!"

Tell your mother it's not your imagination, Milton advised Preston. *She'll believe you.*

"Press, what is it, honey?"

A waiter was already putting menus down on the table, and they took their places there, Brandon holding the chair for his wife, ever the consummate gentleman no matter the situation.

"No more Mr. Make-Believe. Now he's convinced himself he's seeing ghosts," the older Spaulding said in a low voice. "I remember when he was a boy, he had an imaginary friend that lived in the barn. We tried to get him help then, but he was too obstinate to cooperate, remember, Liz?"

"That was play acting, Dad," Preston said cooly, looking up from the matchbooks. Milton endeavored to keep everything calm, knowing that if they were going to explain this to anyone, they would need to do it rationally and methodically. "I was Batman, and I'd pretend that Robin or the Joker was in the barn."

"What's different from your so-called career now? Play acting!"

"I don't understand what you boys are talking about," his mother said.

"May I start you off with drinks?" the waiter asked, awkwardly.

"Do you have Chablis?" Liz asked.

The waiter nodded as Brandon piped up, "I didn't think I'd need it, but a double scotch on the rocks."

Preston, determined to keep his wits about him, considered asking asked for a mocktail, but he opted for a little liquid courage with a vodka and soda. He never forgot how his father reacted with such disappointment, confusion, and anger when Preston had come out to him as a high school senior. This revelation, he reasoned, would have to be easier.

As soon as the waiter left to retrieve their beverages, Preston took a deep breath and tried to succinctly explain the situation.

"Over the past few months, I've been experiencing some strange dreams and a series of coincidences that are...unusual to say the least."

Always a concerned mother, Liz reached out to cover his hand with her own and asked urgently, "Have you seen a doctor? Do you want me to make an appointment for you with someone?"

He slipped his hand out from under hers and Milton made him pat hers, reassuringly.

"This actually started when I went for my physical. I thought it was some kind of anxiety attack at first. There's nothing wrong with me medically, so I've been trying to figure out what triggers it."

"I can tell you what triggers it," Brandon stated, gruffly. "Show business. A whole goddamned industry built around make believe. I'd've paid for any college in the country where a person could pursue a real career."

"Dad, I have suspected this for weeks, but today at the museum confirmed it."

"Confirmed what?"

"It's the Titanic. You could say I have a visceral reaction to things related to the sinking of the ship."

Unlike her husband, Liz was trying to absorb Preston's words with the utmost seriousness.

"Are you studying for a part? Trying to get in character for something?"

Preston and Milton smiled at her appreciatively but tried to explain, "It sounds like that, and it might even make sense if that were the case. But it doesn't have anything to do with my being an actor. I've been doing a lot of reading and research, not just about Titanic but about past lives and reincarnation."

"Christ Almighty, you two. Where's my drink?" Brandon muttered, looking for the waiter.

"I had an art teacher in college who was one hundred percent convinced he was the living embodiment of John Singer Sargent. And I loved Warren Beatty in *Heaven Can Wait*.

Preston snickered a little at his mother's unwavering ability to always give him the benefit of the doubt and was relieved that at least one of his parents was open to listening to him about the possibility.

"Well, I've come to believe that in a past life, I was a passenger aboard the Titanic."

As the waiter arrived with the drinks and began to set them down, Liz leaned in. Her interest was keen, and she asked, "Who do you think you were?"

"The Unsinkable Molly Brown?" Brandon suggested, clutching his scotch and prompting Liz to give him a light, admonishing swat.

"A passenger who did not survive the sinking. He wasn't famous or remarkable enough to be in any of the movies," Preston told them.

I resent being described as unremarkable, Milton told him silently.

"You know what I mean," Preston snapped back, not realizing he was saying it aloud.

Seeing his son actually talking to himself, Brandon just sat back and rolled his eyes before he downed the scotch.

"Would you folks like to hear the specials?" the waiter ventured.

"I think we'll need a few more minutes, please," Liz replied.

"I'll have another scotch while we're waiting," Brandon told him, before adding, "my wife is driving."

Preston continued with his story. "His name was Milton Long from Massachusetts. He was a first-class passenger who drowned."

"Oh, isn't it funny that he would be named Milton," Liz said.

"Why is that funny?" Milton asked, using Preston's voice.

"I'll never forget when you were four years old, and I was registering you to start kindergarten. I was on the phone to the school, and I told them your name repeatedly. I even spelled it for them and the secretary kept thinking I was saying 'Milton.' I assumed she was hard of hearing, and then, on your first day of school when I took you in and the teacher took the attendance, there it was on the class roster:

Milton Spaulding. They even had a cute little name tag for you."

Preston gave his dad an I-told-you-so look and assured his mom, "It still happens to me often."

"And the two names are nothing alike, really. 'Preston' is an old English name we chose from a baby book. You father thought it sounded WASP-y."

Appreciating her enthusiasm for the intrigue, Preston continued.

"Today, when I saw an actual Titanic lifeboat davit at the museum, I was absolutely certain I had touched it before. And I know that, as crazy as it sounds, Milton is a part of me."

"So, you're possessed?" Brandon asked.

"No, Dad, I'm still me. But he's in here, too, if that makes any sense."

"I'm afraid it does not."

Liz did not share her husband's skepticism and proposed, "What do you suppose it means? Shall we make a weekend trip to Massachusetts? Your Aunt Peggy would love that."

"I'm not sure what it means, other than it's a feeling inside of me, and I'm meant to find out why I'm just becoming aware of it now. And maybe there is something

Milton and I are supposed to be doing to help each other. He obviously isn't resting in peace."

"So, it *is* a ghost story…" Brandon concluded.

"Milton's good friend on the ship was from Philadelphia and managed to survive. His name was Jack Thayer, and I'm certain he is connected to the story. Unfortunately, his children and grandchildren have all passed away and their family line ended there."

"You have done your research," Liz remarked, impressed. "Where in Philly did the Thayers live?"

Excited that he had an ally, Preston took the phone out of his breast pocket and looked up the notes he had kept. "The family estate was named Redwood and was on Cheswold Lane in Haverford. I've seen photographs of it, but I don't know if it's still there."

"This is like a scavenger hunt. Or an episode of *Amazing Race*! Let's look for it after lunch on the way home." With a reprimanding look to Brandon, she added, "And before you say anything, since it's my car and I'm driving, you can go along with it or just take the train home."

After thirty-five years of marriage and nearly three decades of fatherhood, Brandon knew when to choose his battles. For the sake of domestic harmony, he had tolerated the follies of Preston's youth with all the plays he'd put on, talent shows he'd entered, and over-the-top Halloween costumes he'd designed, including a Christmas tree and a winged monkey from *The Wizard of Oz*. He had tried to look the other way when his only son had hung boy band posters in his bedroom, when he remembered his own youthful obsession with images of Farrah Fawcett and Lynda Carter.

Preston's rich and immersive fantasy-life delighted his mother but, for Brandon, it went from being an irritation to a serious concern. Brief stints in the Boy Scouts and Little League did nothing to help young Preston make actual three-dimensional friends and Brandon hoped, to no avail, that professional help would allow young Preston to develop more of a "normal" childhood.

In high school, the first time Preston had brought a boy home for dinner that was obviously not a classmate from the Glee Club or the Yearbook Committee, Brandon had tried to make justifications that his son was going through some sort of phase. How much time, money, and attention had he spent over the years trying to persuade Preston to cultivate more manly and mature pursuits? What manifested itself as frustration and impatience was actually a decades-long apprehension for his son's wellbeing and stability.

Other than a surname and some DNA, father and son seemed to have nothing in common, but Brandon kept trying. He loved Preston, in spite of their vast differences, while his fiery wife seemed to love Preston because of them. At least, he consoled himself, his son was showing an interest in something other than musical theater and a promiscuous lifestyle.

After lunch, Liz used her car's GPS system to locate the Thayer family address he'd found for Redwood on the internet. It wasn't far at all, about halfway between Center City and the Paoli train station near the town of Ardmore. Other information he'd uncovered included some black and white photos of a large, stately Tudor and craftsman styled mansion designed by a prominent local architect David Knickerbacker Boyd. It did not look unlike other houses in the area; in fact, it resembled a much larger version of the Spaulding's own house. This one sat on two and a half acres of land with a detached garage/carriage house. It looked picturesque in the photographs, and Milton longed to be there with Jack and his parents. It could have so easily happened if only…

If they'd met sooner. If they'd lived in another time. If Titanic had been sailing more slowly. But there was no one to blame.

"Okay, we're not far now," Liz announced, bringing them to attention. "We're on Gray's Lane, and it shows we're only a quarter mile away." Preston was sitting up front in the passenger seat of the Jaguar while his father dozed in the back. "It should be at the corner of Elbow Lane."

They drove by the massive and impressive looking Merion Cricket Club, sprawled on a twelve-and-a-half-acre property. A simple sign at the entrance proclaimed in elegant cursive, "Established in 1865." Milton remembered that Jack said he'd played cricket, and Preston shivered to think he would certainly have gone there for athletics. They then passed a gigantic recreation center with many tennis courts and a swimming pool, all deserted. There were signs there, too, far less fancy, which read "Permanently Closed."

Liz slowed down and pulled the car onto the side of the road, the sound of gravel crackling beneath the wheels. Brandon stirred in the back seat and looked up to see where they were. Only a few unused, rundown tennis courts remained at the corner where Redwood once stood.

"You're sure of the address?" Liz double checked.

"Yes. Let me hop out for a minute, okay?"

"Take your time, sweetheart."

Preston hoped he and Milton would feel some stirring by being at the site. While the Jaguar idled, they crossed Elbow Lane to further examine the property beyond all the lush greenery. The trees and bushes by the large, standing homes were beautifully manicured but significantly less maintained around the empty tennis center.

A tall and handsome older gentleman walking his dog, a wire fox terrier like the famous Asta in *The Thin Man* movie, appeared from behind some hedges. He was moving slowly and looked to be in his seventies but neatly dressed and even a little dapper.

Let's talk to him, Milton proposed.

"Excuse me, sir," Preston greeted as he approached the man, the dog immediately wagging its tail and pulling at the leash to move in for a scratch, pat, or treat.

"Hattie, down," the man told the dog.

Hattie was my mother's name, Milton said silently, *but I think that may just be coincidence.*

I don't believe in coincidences anymore, Preston mentally told him.

"She's okay," Preston assured the man, aloud, and bending down to greet the canine. "She's a beautiful girl." He knew that flattery might get him somewhere.

"Thank you. She forgets she's an old lady whenever she meets a dog-lover."

Addressing the dog, but for the benefit of the man, Preston said, "Well, if I tell you my name, then I won't be a stranger anymore. Hattie, my name is Milton."

Hattie was licking him affectionately, but still there was no feeling of familiarity with anything.

Standing up and offering his hand to the old man, he introduced himself as "Milton Long."

The man shook his hand and replied, "Dave Bevlock. Getting my steps in. I live down the road. How about you?"

"Visiting the area," Preston told him, employing his best improvisational acting ability. "My family used to know the Thayers. I thought they lived around here in a house called Redwood."

"Oh, that was many, many years ago, I'm afraid. When I was a boy. I don't think any of them are left at all. There were other owners, and then the house was demolished in 2019 to build the tennis courts and parking lot. The Thayers were well known for their connection to the Titanic. The father who worked for the railroad died at sea, but his wife and son made it back."

"I heard that."

"The son married and had children of his own," Mr. Bevlock recounted. "But he never recovered from the trauma. Did you know that he took his own life?"

"Yes. Very sad."

"My wife died young, not long after we were married. I can't imagine someone surviving a tragedy like that, being given a second chance at life, and then just throwing it away."

Milton snapped to attention, ready to defend Jack but Preston was the stronger one at the moment and kept him silent while he simply replied, "We can't know how that would have scarred a person."

Mr. Bevlock shrugged and admitted, "You may have a point. Sorry not to be of more help, Milton."

Milton felt better simply by being addressed by his own name.

Preston thanked him and slowly walked back to the car. Milton was paraphrasing the man's words in their minds. "Imagine being given a second chance at life."

The Spauldings didn't discuss much more about the Titanic or Preston's suspicions once the Redwood lead had dead-ended. The most important thing to him, as far as his parents were concerned, was that he had "come out" about it

to them, and, although his father reacted with a skepticism
and disapproval that shouldn't have surprised him, his
mother had been refreshingly supportive. In a way, they
paralleled the way his friends Greg and Alanna would have
handled it. Although Greg would probably have made a
catty joke about Preston now having to start using
"they/them/theirs" pronouns.

Even so, both Brandon and Liz drove Preston to the
Paoli train station the next midday for his trip back to
Manhattan. As they hugged him simultaneously, Milton
again grateful for the affectionate familial feeling, Liz
reassured her son by saying, "Keep me posted about
everything that happens with Milton. I may do a little
digging around myself, if you don't feel like it's
interfering."

He kissed her soft cheek gratefully, saying "Every
Batman needs his Batgirl. Thank you."

"No thanks necessary. I gave you life. I want you to
enjoy it."

Milton recalled his own mother's protectiveness and
appreciated seeing the quality in Liz.

Brandon pressed three rolled up twenty dollar bills
into his son's hand telling him, "Take yourself out to dinner

when you get back to the City. I'll see if there's anyone in my office who knows any of the Thayer descendants."

Preston was touched and thanked him, too.

As his son stepped away from them, Brandon called after him. "And next time we'll go to an art museum, instead. Maybe I'll find out who I was in a past life!"

God love him, he means well, Milton told Preston.

Once aboard the train, Preston settled into his window seat and thought wistfully about Jack Thayer's sad, suicidal ending. Milton knew Jack would never have been driven to such an action had it not been for the Titanic disaster, whether they had disembarked together in New York or not.

Using his iPhone, Preston resumed more Google searches for "John Borland Thayer, III of Philadelphia" and came across pages of articles and mentions he had already seen, and the usual assortment of now-familiar photographs. All he knew was that Jack had been found in his automobile on the corner of 48th Street and Parkside Avenue, having slashed his own wrists and throat. It was believed that he had been despondent over the death of his son Edward, a bomber pilot, who was shot down in 1943, and his body never recovered. To compound that grief, the following year, on the very anniversary of the Titanic sinking, his beloved and once-merry mother Marian passed away. In spite of having a loving wife and three surviving children, in addition to a distinguished and lucrative career in finance, Jack could not find the strength or purpose to go on living. He was buried at the Church of the Redeemer Cemetery in Bryn Mawr.

The train whizzed past Ardmore and was about to pull in to Philadelphia's 30th Street Station, one of America's most beautiful and bustling transit hubs and not far from the site of Jack's tragic end. There was usually a short wait of two to five minutes there before the train resumed its journey north to New York. While at the stop, Preston's phone tweeted out a Google Alert notification, even though he wasn't aware he had set one up. He reacted to the sound effect and looked at his phone to see what the search engine was sending him.

It was a news item from *The Philadelphia Inquirer* dated Sunday, September 23, 1945, three days after Jack's death. Everyone's iPhones were listening to their users. Maybe they were becoming mind readers, too. The article was accompanied by a photographic portrait of the handsome businessman, unsmiling, in a stylish pinstriped suit and silk necktie. Preston had never seen this before and immediately began to read.

"John B. Thayer III, financial vice president of the University of Pennsylvania and a member of an old Philadelphia family, who had been reported missing since Wednesday, was found dead, his wrists and throat cut, in a parked automobile near the Philadelphia Transit Company loop at 48th Street and Parkside Avenue, yesterday morning. The coroner, one of the first to arrive on the scene after the body was discovered by PTC employees said, Mr. Thayer probably had died forty hours before the body was found at eight fifty in the morning. He believed the death was a suicide."

The train jolted to a rough stop, and Preston looked up from his phone.

"Do you know what I'm thinking?" he asked Milton.

Naturally.

"Let's go."

It was easy to grab a taxi from the long line queued outside the station, and Preston asked to be taken to 48th Street and Parkside Avenue, which was about a ten-minute ride into a rather run-down industrial section of the city. He finished reading the article while they rode.

"Frederick M. Thayer, a brother, and Lieutenant Governor John C. Bell, Jr, a lifelong friend, identified the body at the Morgue. Mr. Bell said that Mr. Thayer had been suffering from a nervous breakdown during the last two weeks, which Mr. Bell explained was due to worrying about the death of his son, who was killed in the service. Mr. Bell said that he had reported Mr. Thayer missing to the state police when the latter failed to return to his home in Grays Lane, Haverford, on Tuesday night."

They had driven right past Gray's Lane just the day before on their way to Redwood. Jack had never moved farther away from his mother than a quarter mile.

"Two PTC employees found the body on the front seat of the car with the feet under the steering wheel. They said they first saw the automobile, a sedan, registered in the name of his wife, Mrs. Lois Thayer, parked on the south side of Parkside Avenue at noon Thursday. When they saw the same car parked there yesterday, they investigated. The car, with Mr. Thayer's body in it, had gone unnoticed by trolley-car passengers and boys who played football nearby. The men, after finding the body, telephoned police who took the body to Presbyterian Hospital."

It was too ghastly to think that Jack had died so gruesomely and alone. And then to remain undiscovered for so long. After what he had managed to survive on April 15, 1912, he couldn't escape the chain of further tragedy and heartache that followed.

"The Deputy Coroner said that there was no doubt that Mr. Thayer used razor blades, which the police found in the car, to kill himself. Dr. Thomas Gates, chairman of the University of Pennsylvania, in a formal statement declared: In the death of Mr. John B. Thayer, we have lost a trusted and loyal servant. He gave unsparingly of himself and had redoubled his efforts in the war period, especially after the death of his son, which was followed closely by the death of his mother. Mr. Thayer's mother, Marian, died at her Haverford home April 14, 1944, which was the 32nd anniversary of her husband's death on the liner Titanic, which sank after striking an iceberg in the Atlantic."

Here the Inquirer's account of the Thayers' experience aboard Titanic was incorrect. It claimed that "Mrs. Thayer was placed in a lifeboat with her younger son, Frederick (who was not on board at all), while John stood with his father on the Titanic's deck when the ship went down. The younger Thayer was rescued."

There was no mention whatsoever of Jack's heroism in floating beside, and eventually atop, a flimsy collapsible lifeboat until the Carpathia rescue ship appeared hours later. And again, Milton's presence alongside his friend had been erased from the account altogether. The rest of the article delved into his military, professional, and philanthropic achievements, as well as mentioning his various club memberships and his hobby, figure skating. Milton remembered them discussing winter sports and his own pre-voyage holiday to St. Moritz. How Jack had wanted to hear the full story of Milton's playful deceit about his age while there. How he longed to be able to finish that yarn and enjoy their togetherness.

The cab came to a stop. Even though there was a narrow stretch of lawn on one side of the street, it was a derelict looking area. The grizzled driver looked back at Preston and asked, "Are you sure this is where you want to get out?"

He had a point, Preston thought. This didn't look like the kind of neighborhood where he wanted to be stranded, even in the middle of a sunny summer Sunday.

"Do you mind waiting for me while I walk outside for a moment? I'm looking for something, but I won't be more than five minutes."

The driver wasn't sure how to answer, so Preston handed him one of the rolled up twenty dollar bills from his father.

"Five minutes. You can keep the meter running. I'll leave my duffle bag here with you, so you know I'm coming back."

"Okay, man."

Preston stepped out onto the cracked pavement and hoped the taxi driver was a man of his word, especially with his luggage in the back seat. He began to walk along the sidewalk, waiting to sense something of Jack's presence here.

He continued on for less than a minute when, even though the sun was beating down on him, he felt an intense pain that felt like a thousand knives stabbing into every inch of body. It was instantaneous and unexpected, causing him to double over. Preston managed not to fall to his knees, for fear that the cab would speed away at any sign of trouble. What was happening?

Milton immediately recognized the feeling. It was the exact sensation he felt when his body hit the icy waters under which he disappeared. His death had been so swift he hadn't even realized it at the time, but now it came back to him.

It had to be here, Preston, Milton told him, trying to bolster him from his pained position.

Preston managed to stiffen his spine and take a look at his surroundings while he felt the cold needles continue to pierce his psyche.

They saw a horrifying, grisly flash of fifty-year-old Jack in his wife's sedan, just as he would have appeared to the men who discovered him—bled out and rotting from exposure. His eyes and mouth were wide open in grotesque desperation and agony.

Preston was terrified but Milton prevented him from screaming or even turning away. Milton, unafraid of death after not even knowingly experiencing his own, forced Preston to resist outwardly reacting.

Milton did this by calling upon whatever strength and willpower he possessed to disallow this frightening image from overtaking their minds. The pain started to dissipate, and the frigid feeling was quickly replaced with searing heat from the sun, and Preston was soon soaked in a cold sweat from head to toe.

The horrible sight of dead Jack in the car dissipated along with the pain, and they had a momentary glimpse of Jack as he appeared on the deck of the Titanic before he leapt overboard—handsome, young, and stoic. He was again telling Milton exactly what he'd said then, "I'll be with you in a minute."

"I'll see you in New York," Milton replied.

"I can't wait," Jack said once again as he had in 1912, before vanishing.

Milton wanted to bring Jack back again but not here. Not where it had ended so horrifically for him. Preston, exhausted, managed to turn around and walk back to the taxi, albeit unsteadily.

Chapter Eight

"If you're going to tell me tales from *The Twilight Zone* this early in the day, I need to switch to vodka," Greg quipped before flagging down the waitress and ordering a Kettle One martini.

"Make it two," Marcus chimed in, visibly dumbfounded. "You've been living on Edgar Allan Poe Street too long, Preston."

Preston arranged for an afternoon brunch in the private dining cellar of Harlem's popular Clay restaurant. He had asked the kindly owner, Andrea, to make sure they remained undisturbed, as he had an important matter to discuss with his three closest friends.

Setting it up as sort of an "intervention in reverse," Preston wanted to explain and update the situation he was experiencing, and, hopefully, they would understand why he'd been behaving so out of character lately. Maybe even believe him.

Alanna wasn't drinking, and neither was Preston, determined to keep clear-headed and not allow the others to think that his encounters with Milton and Jack were somehow alcohol—or some other substance—induced.

"Cut him some slack, guys," Alanna advised. "He's not making this up."

"Come off it. If he's not haunted or possessed, then he's schizophrenic," said Marcus.

"Baby, you have got to snap out of it," Greg told Preston, seriously concerned. "Or talk to a doctor. Let me refer you to my shrink…"

Preston reached across the table and touched Greg's hand in a show of earnest friendship. "Other than telling you that the Armani suit you wore to your sister's wedding made you look thin, have I ever lied to you?"

"Bitch."

"Press, why do you think this would be happening to you now, all of a sudden?" Alanna asked.

"It's not all of a sudden. The clues have always been there, my whole life. But the puzzle pieces are starting to come together."

"Or, it's all just a series of coincidences," Greg suggested.

"Why can't a coincidence also be a clue? Maybe Milton has always been a part of me, just waiting to emerge."

"Better late than never," Marcus said, dripping with sarcasm.

"That's what he said," Preston responded, surprising them with such candor that they knew he truly believed it. "But he didn't manifest himself until I needed him."

"Why would you think you need him?"

"Think about it. I've been adrift for years. With relationships, my career. It was a self-destructive path with the sex and the drugs and the booze…"

Marcus teased his boyfriend by asking Greg, "And what's your excuse, pray tell?"

Preston continued on, determined to make his point even if they couldn't yet see it. "The last time I got hammered, Milton actually appeared to me in the mirror to tell me how disappointed he was in me. In my stupor, I'd applied online to the Woods Hole Oceanographic Institute, and they sent me back an application addressed to Milton Long."

"Classic blackout behavior," Marcus said, dismissively.

Alanna delicately mentioned, "In rehab I learned about dissociative amnesia. It makes people unable to recall stressful or traumatic events."

As the waitress arrived with the martinis, Preston argued, "This is just the opposite. I'm actually *recalling* events. And what could be more stressful or traumatic than drowning on the Titanic?"

Having overheard a snippet of his statement, the waitress set down the drinks and quickly stepped away.

Greg took a healthy swig from his martini and turned suddenly serious.

"How does it work? Can you just switch Milton on and off? Is he listening to us now?"

Preston took a long pause to consider this, hoping Milton would come up with the right answer. The others looked at him, expectantly.

Milton asked Preston, *Why is any of this their concern?*

Preston ignored that and offered, "We're still figuring it out. But his life was cut short, so he's getting another shot, in a way."

"What about *your* life, "Alanna asked.

Preston shrugged and admitted, "So far, he's a pretty good influence."

Milton began to speak through Preston, careful to refer to himself in the third person so as not to frighten or worry them.

"He was searching for purpose in a time where he was unable to express his true self. His personal desires and ambitions were squelched. Therefore, so too were his professional ones."

The cadence of Preston's voice along with the syntax and vocabulary he was using were quite clearly those of another person, and the friends realized Milton was speaking to them.

"For all his education and privilege, he never discovered a passion. The death certificate listed him as a gentleman of leisure. What kind of epitaph is that for a twenty-nine-year-old man? Through some miracle of fate or magic or God, Milton needs to finally experience the life he was deprived of living, while Preston can still live a fulfilling and happy one of his own."

"And what will that take?" Alanna finally asked, unsure of whom she was addressing.

Preston and Milton answered in unison, "That's what we have to figure out."

Greg, like the others, was paying such close attention that he was scrambling to make mental notes of everything coming out of Preston's mouth, but one detail in particular had caught his attention. Milton's age at the time of his death.

"Twenty-nine, the same as you."

As simple and unsurprising as it was to Preston and Milton, it stunned the others when he replied, "And the same birthday, October 19th."

Greg pounced on it, lightening the mood. "How long have I been begging you to let me plan your thirtieth? At least now we have a theme!"

Preston still could have cared less about his birthday, which was still months away, but Milton thought this frivolous friend may have a point.

Back in his apartment later that afternoon, Preston was relieved that he'd been able to unburden himself without having his friends commit him to a psych ward. He also conceded to let them plan his birthday bash with the caveat that he'd have final approval of the details. He'd had enough surprises lately.

I think that went rather well, Milton told him.

"Better than I expected," Preston admitted. "Greg and Marcus can be a tough audience."

Thank you for letting me speak freely, Preston. After what we went through in Philadelphia and talking with your friends, I'm convinced I know the appropriate next steps.

Having abstained all through their brunch, Preston was ready for a glass of wine, moved to the refrigerator to select a bottle, and said, "By all means, enlighten me."

I say this with respect and affection...

"Uh oh. I sense a *but* coming."

From my own experience, I have to agree with your parents about finding an alternative to your show business pursuits. Even if it's just something to stimulate and challenge in the meantime. Going to Equinox and nightclubs is not the answer. That's the precise equivalent to my rambling around Europe as a bon vivant.

"But you enrolled in both Columbia and Harvard without satisfaction."

Much to my eternal chagrin. I'm here to help you avoid the mistakes I made. Find purpose. You take voice lessons, so why not further expand your studies? For God's sake, this is the New York City of today. And you live down the street from Columbia University!

Even if there was no hiding anything from him, Preston was irritated to admit that Milton was right. His father had often mentioned their prestigious non-degree programs.

Milton felt marvelously unburdened now, almost giddy with the liberty to express himself to Preston.

He went on and urged, *And call Todd. Remember what the man with the dog named Hattie said about second chances? Not everyone gets one.*

Preston felt sorry for Milton and ashamed of himself. Milton actually cared about him beyond just being the body he'd been divinely assigned to inhabit.

Milton went on, *Your carousel of casual encounters is unhealthy and will never lead to anything satisfying. You don't seem to appreciate the freedom you have to actually pursue a meaningful relationship with someone of the same gender. It was all but impossible for me.*

Again, he was right, Preston knew. He took his many advantages for granted. What had the Stonewall riots and all the subsequent work of the gay liberation movement been for, if not to allow the LGBTQ+ community to enjoy the same rights as their heterosexual counterparts? "Gay Pride" had been born out of rising above "societal shame."

Having uncorked a cold bottle of Pinot Grigio, Preston poured himself a glass and took a satisfying sip.

Do it for me, Milton argued, *and you'll be doing it for yourself, as well.*

Feeling a kinship between them that allowed for playfulness, he asked, "If I do, will you leave me alone?"

If you do, maybe I'll leave you altogether.

Such a possibility hadn't occurred to Preston. He grew accustomed to the idea that Milton would now be a permanent part of his life and psyche. He realized he liked it.

That night, Preston sat up in bed unable to sleep even with the white noise machine quietly humming. He went through the vicious cycle of scrolling through Instagram to help him relax and drift off but instead getting distracted by multiple account postings. A few months ago, the algorithms always fed him content from hunky male models, body builders, and porn stars. Nowadays, though, it was a steady stream of ocean liner fan pages, Titanic memorabilia, and Edwardian fashion. He swiped his index finger up and up, browsing.

When I needed to fall asleep, I used to pick up a book, Milton remarked.

"I used to pick up something else," Preston muttered.

I don't suppose you'd have any interest in Ethan Frome?

Preston let out a heavy sigh and asked, "Did you read a lot?"

I was never without a book. Like you're never without your phone.

An Instagram ad popped up from Columbia University. It caught Milton's attention, and he urged Preston, *Look at that one.*

Preston obliged as he said, "I should walk up to the campus, so you can see how it's changed."

The Columbia post was touring their program for non-degree students. "Registration is open for adult, non-degree students seeking to enhance skills, pursue person and professional interests, or explore new disciplines without committing to a full degree program."

Milton spoke again. *Did you mean it when you told your mates I was a good influence on you?*

Preston scrolled down further to read that available courses included computer science, religion, public affairs, and broadcast journalism.

※※※

Having effectively ghosted Todd, Preston knew he'd have to work a little harder to convince him to see each other again. Milton suggested a grand gesture. but not one that would risk scaring him off altogether.

Knowing that Todd finished up at the medical practice at six, he decided to take a shot and wait outside the entrance at that time, bearing a gift and a mea culpa. He swung by the Shakespeare and Company bookstore on Broadway and 69th Street and bought a brand-new coffee table book that profiled the great MGM Movie musicals of Hollywood's Golden Years. Along with that, once he got closer to the doctor's office, he purchased a small but colorful bouquet of brilliant red peonies, wrapped in brown parchment paper, and tied with a simple straw ribbon. By five fifty he was on the sidewalk looking like a dutiful suitor.

He hadn't counted on the sudden summer rainstorm that had been nowhere in the forecast and seemed to blow over Manhattan in a matter of minutes. Before he risked getting drenched or struck by the wild bolts of lightning that were flashing over the city skyline, Preston ducked inside the building's lobby to wait it out in safety.

The rain continued to pound for another ten minutes, with several other people taking cover or waiting it out alongside him. Then, as quickly as it had blown in, the storm moved on, and clouds parted to bathe everything in golden, late-afternoon sunshine. Just as Preston was about to step back outside, one of the elevators opened its doors, and

Todd emerged, still in his blue scrubs and seeming to be in a rush. The two men surprised each other, coming face-to-face right there by the bank of elevators.

Todd paused long enough to say, "Oh, hey."

"You look like you're in a rush. I don't want to keep you, but…"

"And you look like you're on the way to a date," Todd said, nodding at the flowers.

"That's what I'm hoping for, anyway," Preston replied, extending his gifts toward Todd. "If you'll accept my apology. I've had a lot going on. But that doesn't give me the excuse for being a dickhead, and I'm truly sorry."

Did you have to use vulgarity? Milton asked Preston silently.

"A jerk. I was a jerk," Preston backtracked.

Todd couldn't help but smile and ushered them away from the elevators, out of the way of people trying to exit the lobby.

He took the flowers from Preston and said, "I love peonies, thank you. I don't remember the last time someone gave me flowers."

Offering him the book, Preston said, "I thought you'd like this, too. I promise, there isn't a single Titanic reference in there."

Now smiling wider as he took the book and examined the cover, Todd said, "Are you sure? Debbie Reynolds did *The Unsinkable Molly Brown* in 1964 and that was MGM."

"Oh, shit!"

Again, profanity? Milton scolded. *You need to work on that, Preston.*

"It's great, thanks," Todd said. "And I accept your apology, of course."

"I think I was having some sort of pre-birthday anxiety about my thirtieth. My best friend has been pressuring me to do something extravagant and wild instead of just going out for dinner, which I'd much prefer."

"Milestone years can freak some people out," Todd acknowledged.

"So, I'm trying to turn over a new leaf. Settle down a bit."

"And watch that blood pressure?"

Preston nodded, adding, "I'm also going back to school, in a way. I decided to sign up for a continuing education summer session at Columbia. Broadcast journalism."

"That's awesome. You'd be a great reporter. Smart and passionate. Photogenic."

"You're too kind, Todd. I hope kind enough to give me another chance to go out sometime."

"I'd love that. I'm meeting some friends tonight, and I'm already late. Why don't I text you tomorrow, and we'll figure something out?"

"That would be wonderful," Preston answered, feeling himself blush.

Clutching the gifts, Todd gave him a peck on the cheek and said, "Thank you again for these. And for coming all the way down here to see me."

Just as he was about to hurry out the door, Todd stopped to look right into Preston's grayish-blue eyes and add, "You're a true gentleman."

You can thank me for that, Milton thought.

Todd was correct about Preston's innate talent for broadcasting. He was almost immediately teacher's pet in the class of two dozen students for the university's "Modern Media Journalism" course, which promised them opportunities to "learn the industry practices and basic skills needed to produce news stories across audio, visual, and digital mediums covering everything from an overview of investigative tools and techniques, to interviewing skills, journalistic ethics, storytelling, and using social media for news gathering, distribution, and building your personal brand."

Halfway through the six-week program, Preston had already broken out as the star of the class, was instinctively able to master the curriculum, and execute the assignments. His talents as a performer meshed well with requisite skills, like using earpieces with IFB transmissions, microphones, teleprompters, green screen chroma-keys, as well as composing and editing content—all of which came remarkably easy to him after all the time he'd spent on commercial sets and on-camera TV auditions. Milton silently helped by contributing his natural articulation and Ivy-league trained ability to focus. Consequently, Preston impressed all of the guest instructors, who were esteemed professionals in their various journalistic fields, and most importantly, the main professor—a bookish but charismatic retired network anchorman named Wallace Grant. He was a barrel chested African American man of about 70, with a buttery baritone, commanding presence, and air of authority. He and Preston hit it off immediately.

Preston recognized him from his ubiquitous presence on television news and appreciated his almost fraternal approach to teaching, beginning with his insistence that students address him by his first name.

"Were you ever an actor, Wallace?" Preston ventured to ask one day after class.

Looking surprised, his teacher answered, "As a matter of fact, that was my original career path after a few semesters in my college dramatic society. What made you suspect?"

"Your voice. You sound like you could be a speech coach. I bet you never needed a microphone to project to the back row."

Flattered but feigning modesty, Wallace admitted, "No, I did not. In fact, my wife is always telling me to tone down the volume."

"Same here. One of my homeroom teachers in high school actually nicknamed me 'Loud Mouth.'"

Wallace had a hunch about Preston's untapped on-air skills that went beyond good looks. His enthusiastic student struck him as an "old soul" and was proving to have an innate ability to simply be himself on both sides of the lens. It had been the secret to his own success, and he recognized it in Preston Spaulding.

Preston even deleted all the existing content from his cherished Instagram and Tik Tok accounts that featured images of him partying in Fire Island and the Hamptons, camping it up with Greg and Marcus, or sipping champagne

in glamorous locations. Now, his six thousand followers
would have to make do with his thoughts on local politics,
images of newsmaking celebrities and politicians that linked
to the new blog he had started, as well as a series of polls he
had branded "What Do You Think?" concentrating on
various social issues around the New York City area. At
first, he saw a big drop off in followers but was steadily
regrowing that number with new, more astute social media
users.

All the while, Preston and Todd began to see each
other again regularly. Not every night, and not every date
ended in sex. There were dinners, movies, and nightclubs,
but there were also simpler pleasures, such as picnics in
Central Park and trips to many of Manhattan's world-class
museums of art, history, fashion, and design. Preston had
never before been so captivated by a person's mind in
addition to their physical prowess. One day they would take
a Peloton class together, and the next they'd be on an
architectural tour of the Cathedral of St. John the Divine. A
fancy five-course feast at Nougatine was much more
expensive, but no more fun than a couple of slices and Diet
Cokes from Little Italy Pizza. Todd was truly a modern-day
Renaissance man and Preston, too, was proving to exhibit
new sides to himself with all he was learning through his

studies. Summer was a traditionally slow time for the show business industry, so there were few auditions to attend, and Preston was happy to devote his days to school and most evenings to Todd.

His supportive parents and friends noticed his evolution, too, and were cautiously optimistic that he was on his way to a more stable and settled lifestyle. None of them, not even his doting mother or inquisitive best friend, dared to mention anything about the Titanic or Milton, lest they risk throwing him off kilter from his progress. And any time Preston felt an urge to fall back into bad habits, Milton was comfortable and present enough to steer him back on the right back.

Milton and Preston made a good team.

Professor Grant announced to his students what their assignment would be in lieu of a final exam. They were to produce, shoot, and edit a three-minute video segment suited to a national network news program on any subject of their choosing, provided it was considered as having appeal to a broad demographic of viewers and that the student appear on camera as the reporter/interviewer. Preston was practically salivating at the prospect and couldn't wait to get started.

It would be due in a fortnight, and he asked Milton if he thought it would be all right to confer with Todd about the story he would cover. Todd possessed a natural empathic quality and a knack for listening that rivaled Alanna's.

Of course, Milton told him, touched that his opinion was being sought. He was growing increasingly fond of Todd and the relationship Preston was slowly building with him. *That's what true partnerships are all about*, he'd advised. He thought of his own parents and how, even though it was customary in their time for the man to make all the important decisions, they rarely acted on anything without mutual consultation and discussion.

Preston excitedly texted Todd, asking if they could meet at a cozy little Thai place he knew in Morningside Heights. There they could talk quietly, and, between appointments, Todd replied that he could make it there by seven, and if he was running late, to order some Shumai dumplings. Milton tried to avoid weighing in but secretly hoped that whatever story topic Preston would choose would have a medical angle to it, so that Todd could somehow participate. Preston definitely had something in mind but managed to use his volition to keep from letting it slip even to Milton.

When Todd arrived at Thai Kitchen on Amsterdam Avenue, a piping hot plate of pork and shrimp dumplings had just been placed on the table in front of Preston. They greeted each other happily with a quick but tender kiss on the lips before Todd quickly used some hand sanitizer so he could begin enjoying their appetizer. He was famished.

The food was hotter than he expected, burning his mouth, and Todd was forced to chew with an open mouth and take a swallow of water to wash it down. They laughed about it, and Preston said, "Whoa, slow down there, big fella."

Todd scooted his chair around so that they could sit side by side. Preston leaned over and bestowed another kiss on him, then licked his lips saying, "Mmm, spicy."

Giving Preston's thigh a squeeze, Todd said back, "*You're* spicy. What's got you in such a good mood? What did you want to talk about?"

While they awaited their Thai iced teas, Preston enthusiastically shared the details of his final course assignment and how he couldn't wait to get to work on it immediately the next morning. The truth was the only reason he hadn't already begun his research was because he was waiting to talk to Todd before he allowed himself to spring it on Milton.

Still touching his leg, Todd told him, "Whatever got you to turn over this new leaf is really working for you, Press. It's great to see you so happy and passionate about things. And it's also very sexy, I have to say."

"I hope you'll still think so when I tell you my idea. It's Titanic related."

Milton suddenly felt a sense of dread he hadn't experienced in weeks. Where was Preston going with this?

Good natured as ever, Todd simply smiled and said, "Go ahead. I can take it."

"As you know, my interest in the Titanic story is more historical than about the movies, but I just missed the official Titanic Convention held in Pigeon Forge, Tennessee. That's very all-encompassing and brings together enthusiasts from all aspects of her story and the genre."

"Gosh, I'm sorry we missed it," Todd said, dripping with sarcasm.

"But..." he began with a big build-up, "...I read that there is an event for a fan club of James Cameron's movie coming up next weekend just outside of Boston. A screening, a costume contest, and an autograph session with some of the actors from the film."

"I don't get it. You said you weren't drawn to the dramatizations..."

"That's why I can be objective and cover it as a human interest story. And I may not be a fan, but as they say on that podcast, there is no shortage of Titaniacs who are! And they take it very seriously. Imagine juxtaposing the hardcore fans and all their passion with the visuals and pageantry of the event."

Todd considered it for a moment before admitting, "I actually went to a Hollywood autograph show once in Paramus, New Jersey. My aunt wanted to go because there were a bunch of old TV stars from *Dynasty* and *The Love Boat* who charged ten bucks a pop to sign autographs or pose for pictures with admirers. It was kind of a hoot."

"See?"

Milton was relieved that Todd was accepting the idea. Maybe more so than he was.

Todd continued, "I remember thinking how cool it was to see Barbara Eden from *I Dream of Jeannie* and George Takei from *Star Trek*, in person. Lieutenant Sulu was always my favorite character.

"I think it would be a great specialty piece, whether someone is a Titanic fan or not. Everybody can identify with what it's like to have a pop culture hobby, whether it's horror or sci-fi or NASCAR..."

"I get it, I get it. You don't have to sell me."

"Maybe I do. Maybe I still need to sell myself, since you and I are still getting to know each other."

"…and enjoying every minute of it."

"If it's not too much, too soon to ask. Will you come with me? It's just a weekend. We could take Amtrak up to Boston."

"Do I have to wear a costume?"

"No, but you can help me with the gear."

"Aren't there very strict union laws for crews?" he kidded, popping another dumpling in his mouth now that they were cooler.

Preston discreetly put his hand between Todd's leg and gave a rub that brought him immediately to aroused attention.

"Oh, I intend to pay you for your services, sir."

Milton didn't necessarily enjoy this kind of demonstrative affectionate activity in public, but he found that, more and more, he liked Preston and Todd together, in and out of the bedroom.

On the train to Boston, Preston and Todd nuzzled together and looked through the details of the *Titanic* film fan event on Todd's iPad. "All Aboard the Ship of Dreams Weekend" it proclaimed with photographs of mega-fans

costumed as characters from the film. There was a Jack, a
Rose, a Cal, a Captain Smith, and a drag queen dressed as
Molly Brown. Milton saw the entire thing as a tasteless
mockery but recognized that it could be a means to an end in
his desire for them both to find some ultimate fulfillment.
And even if the 1997 blockbuster was a bastardized version
of the Titanic story, it was still compelling, entertaining, and
a significant bonding experience.

"I think this is going to be hysterical," Todd
admitted. "We'll probably be the only ones not in costume."

Preston had called the organizers to register and
shared his plans to make a documentary-style news segment
he was hoping to shop around to local news outlets. If
nothing else, he would happily share it with them for their
YouTube channel, and they unhesitatingly gave him two
complimentary entries as "Press" passes. It made him feel
very official, and Todd was charmed by how dedicated
Preston was to the project and the obvious pleasure it was
already bringing him.

Todd's boyish, affable personality combined with his
altruistic commitment to his work in health care had already
won over Preston, as well. The last several weeks had
brought them closer together, and it was the first time he'd
captured a simultaneous sense of sexual attraction and

affection. It felt good and he wondered why it had taken him so long to experience. Milton, too, was gratified. If he couldn't have had it for himself during his own life, he was getting to experience it now through Preston.

Todd Hafkin was a quality guy, which was plain for anyone to see. Preston resolved not to take him for granted and risk blowing such a good thing. As much as he confided in his close friends, Todd was probably the most trustworthy person he knew to be able to go along with all this without judgement or reproach. Preston felt that he could tell him anything. So, he would.

As the train barreled closer to Boston Station, Preston made the decision to fully disclose his link to Milton. If he was keen to participate in the fan event and hadn't been scared away by his previous meltdown in the movie theater, Todd would have an open mind. After all, he had said as much back at Thai Kitchen when he told Preston, "I can take it.". Milton wasn't as sure but by now he had come to better trust his host's judgement, and he could always jump in with an assist, if necessary.

Careful to couch the revelation with a casual, humorous air, Preston began, "If you think dressing up as Kate Winslet is silly, do you want to know something really far out?"

Todd wasn't addled in the least, thinking that Preston's Titanic mania was actually kind of adorable. "I'm listening."

"I appreciate that you are a clinical thinker, being in medicine and all. And that you also are a very good sport, going along with me on this adventure."

"I can't wait to see you in action, Press."

"I'm hoping you'll keep an open mind when I tell you that circumstances since that night at the Waverly have led me to believe I have a deeper connection to Titanic than you might think."

"Deeper? Is that a pun?" Todd smiled, encouraging Preston to feel more relaxed.

"I discovered my past life. One that ended when Titanic sank."

Preston paused, waiting for Todd to react in some wide-eyed way as Greg or his father had, but the handsome nurse just shrugged, nonplussed, and said, "I stand by what I said then, not everything can be explained. I still believe that."

Treading carefully, Preston continued, "I figured out who I was. Who I still am, sort of. I don't want to freak you out, but I know this person is inside of me."

Good humored but without satire, Todd spoke just as carefully and said, "Whoever it is, they appear to be having a very wonderful influence on you."

Preston nodded to admit that Todd was correct. "That's all Milton."

"Milton, eh? Not the most attractive name I've ever heard. But do I have him to thank for our seeing each other again?"

Preston nodded again.

Todd leaned over and put his forehead up against Preston's in a loving gesture before asking, "Does this make us a throuple?"

Preston leaned back and laughed heartily. What a perfect response. Any other guy would have jumped right off the train.

"He really likes you. We both do."

Confessing to having noticed the framed photo in Preston's bedroom, Todd asked, "Is that Milton on your nightstand? With the ears?"

"No, that was his friend, Jack Thayer. I've become convinced theirs was an unrequited love."

"I would imagine most gay romances remained unrequited back then."

Preston and Milton were both touched by his empathy and understanding.

"Today's world is a bit of shit show," Todd said. "But even so, I'm glad we're living in these times and not back then."

He then surprised them both when he added, "This one's for Milton," and leaned in to plant a soft, lingering kiss. Preston felt like he was melting as Milton yielded to the sensation of Jack's mouth on his.

From the Boston Amtrak station, they took a rideshare to the nearby Holiday Inn Express Hotel serving as the host venue for the *Titanic* fan event. Checking in was an experience in itself. The place was crawling with attendees of every age, demographic, and walk of life…all brethren because of their common ardor. The lobby was decorated with posters from the film and a huge Styrofoam iceberg right next to a cardboard replica of the ship's bow immortalized by Kate Winslet and Leonardo DiCaprio in their romantic flying scene. People were taking turns posing for selfies with these props, and Todd whispered to Preston, "You only take me to the best places."

"And the event doesn't even kick off until tonight," Preston laughed. "Let's drop our stuff in the room and then start getting some footage and interviews with these folks."

Preston would begin with approaching fans for vox pops, impromptu man-on-the-street style questions that can be edited into thematic sound bites. He had a professional microphone connected to his iPhone, which Todd manned in the capacity of cameraman.

Most people were not only excited to be attending but eager to talk and share their passion for the film and its soap-operatic mixture of romance and disaster. He would ask, "What does the film *Titanic* mean to you?" and within an hour, he had dozens of animated responses.

"My mom wouldn't let me watch it until I was eight, but I've probably seen it at least five hundred times since. I can recite every line."

"Oh my god, *Titanic* means everything to me. I collect the VHS tapes, the DVDs, and now I'm working on my Blu-ray collection."

"I just love Leo and Kate. They're the perfect couple. Every time I watch it, I keep hoping he won't die."

"It has everything. It's the perfect movie."

"Cal is so sexy. I mean, he's awful and mean, but come on. He's gorgeous."

"If I had the chance, I'd go on that ship. I'd just make sure to get on a lifeboat early."

"Leo didn't need to die. She could have made room for him on that floating door. Well, actually, it was a panel."

"Every time I see it, I cry. No movie has ever made me cry, except *Titanic*."

"I've seen the alternate ending. They should have gone with that one. But I still like it."

"I could watch it every day. Whenever it's on TV, I stop what I'm doing to watch."

It was a bottomless well of sound bites.

"I'm wearing the limited edition *Titanic* perfume. Would you like to smell me?"

"Some zillionaire is building a Titanic II. I'd do anything to sail on that ship."

"Did you know Leo wasn't the first casting choice? Can you imagine if Jared Leto or Matthew McConaughey got the part?"

"How cool is it when the ship breaks apart? By today's standards, the special effects are sketchy. But even so, wow!"

Milton wondered if these people even realized there was an actual tragedy behind the melodramatic story they watched on screen. People died. Hundreds and hundreds and hundreds of people. And those who lived, like Jack, were never the same again. As Jack had written in his own memoir, "In my mind, the world of today awoke April 15, 1912."

The most solemn item on the evening agenda, printed on bright yellow flyers posted around the hotel, would be a candlelight vigil held outside at the swimming pool in memory of James Cameron's longtime producing partner, *Titanic* producer Jon Landau, who had passed away in July after a battle with cancer.

After a cash-bar cocktail hour to give attendees the opportunity to meet and greet each other, the evening event would kick off with a screening of the film. Everyone was encouraged to dress as their favorite characters, and afterwards, there would be a costume parade, with a local historian and distant ancestor of a Titanic steerage passenger serving as judges. The grand prize would be a copy of the latest Blu-ray edition of the film and a genuine period replica of a White Star life vest.

Preston filmed audience reactions during the screening which included, as expected, everything from open-mouthed wonder, to gasps of horror, as well as some cheers and tears. After Celine Dion's "My Heart Will Go On" and the final credits rolled, the houselights were brought up and a gentleman in a perfectly tailored officer's uniform came to stand before the movie screen and announce, "And now, ladies and gentlemen, friends and fans, our annual *Titanic* costume competition. Entrants may now proceed here, on our own little Promenade Deck."

James Horner's instrumental film soundtrack began to play, and, one by one, two dozen participants strutted their stuff to supportive and enthusiastic applause from the assembled audience. The first was a plus-sized drag queen decked out as Kathy Bates' Molly Brown character but looking more like a community theater version of Dolly Levi.

"You shine up like a new penny," she shouted to the delight of fans, quoting the screenplay line.

She must be rolling in her grave, Milton told Preston, who was expertly manning the camera to pan the room for crowd reactions.

The winning costume was a plump middle-aged lady who had expertly recreated the boarding attire worn by Frances Fisher as Ruth. She even had a perfectly styled red wig to match the one worn in the film. Preston was certain the title would have gone to a Floridian real estate agent named Gary, who was a dead ringer for DiCaprio's heartthrob protagonist. Milton thought the runner up, a doppelgänger for Captain Smith, was the deserving winner.

Preston agreed and confided to the gentleman, "You got robbed, Captain."

The zaftig woman, who took the top prize, was so overwhelmed with her victory that she was nearly sobbing like a Miss Universe pageant queen when the uniformed emcee presented her with a prize: a signed copy of James Cameron's book, *Ghosts of the Abyss*.

"Now you'll never have to worry about working as a seamstress, Ruth," he quipped in reference to one of the character's most memorable lines from the film.

The audience laughed, leaving Preston, Milton, and Todd charmed by the high spirits and fellowship of the assembled fans.

Preston and Todd looked over the next day's schedule. The morning would feature a lecture by the historian, a swap meet of merchandise, and a special autograph session with two of the minor actors from the film and two authors of *Titanic*-related books. There would be an afternoon matinee screening of the film, just for good measure, followed by a special supper recreated from Titanic's final dinner menu. Naturally, a string quartet would accompany the meal with period music.

"Impressive," Todd admitted, reading the rundown. The musicians were all guest artists from the Boston Symphony Hall Orchestra.

The final item on the agenda would be a special screening of a recent documentary about the making of the film that included behind-the-scenes insight from Cameron's cast and crew. Entitled *Ship of Dreams: Titanic Movie Diaries*, the director, an exuberant British actress named Alexandra Boyd who appeared briefly in Cameron's film, would follow that with a question-and-answer session. Preston had run into her while he was setting up his tripod in the screening area, and they had spoken briefly.

"She's great talent with a big personality and an expressive face. I'll have to interview her, too," Preston noted.

"Sounds like a full day," Todd remarked. "We'd better rest up."

As they schlepped all the gear back upstairs, Preston was compelled to acknowledge Todd, "You're a very good sport. I'm really grateful for you all your help."

Pausing from fumbling with his armload of equipment, Todd looked him in the eye with a sweet sincerity, and said, "Don't you get it by now? I'm loving this time with you."

The trip had already bonded them, and the men got very little rest that night, in spite of all the hours they spent in bed. The Holiday Inn Express might have had a meager Yelp rating but, for them, it felt five stars.

Nestled in their raggedy third-floor room overlooking the parking lot, Preston and Todd made love for hours in spite of how weary they were from their long day. Maybe it was all that running around that allowed Preston to relax himself into the coupling with a feeling of ease and abandon.

Without any need of artificial enhancement or stimulant, he found their sexual compatibility was the only boost his libido needed and dared to admit to himself that he couldn't remember the last time he'd had sober sex. Their bodies came together, and it was romantic and passionate. Even fun. And certainly romantic. This was a first for Preston.

Milton dared to indulge himself and imagine that Todd was actually Jack's lithe, strong, unclothed body clinging to him. A first for Milton.

The next day was indeed a full one, shooting great content, which Preston would periodically upload from his phone onto his laptop. He and Todd had initially assumed that "fan" was just an abbreviation for "fanatic", and they would encounter quirky oddballs to easily play up for comedic effect. Milton tried to keep an open mind, and it soon became apparent that the people participating in the event were all there to have some good, clean fun and came from all walks of life...united by their affection and devotion to the now-classic motion picture.

For the themed meal, a well-known author of Titanic-themed cookbooks, Veronica Hinke, had provided organizers with easy-to-replicate recipes from her collection, including salmon mousseline, consommé jardinière, a spring pea truffle soufflé, and red-wine poached figs.

Not a bad effort, Milton admitted.

That gave Preston the brainstorm to enlist some of the attendees in a taste test to share the reactions.

As Preston and Todd were moving around the banquet hall, Todd was surprised to bump into a guy he knew from nursing school. Nick, it turned out, had traveled from Philadelphia where he'd moved to get his medical degree at Jefferson Medical University. It was a reunion as happy as it was unexpected.

"Toddy, how did I never know you were a Titanic nut, too?" he asked, jovially. "I'd've dragged your ass to the museum experience in Pigeon Forge."

"I'm not one of you," he laughed. "Or at least not until this weekend. Maybe I'm becoming a new convert. I'm helping out with a video shoot."

"Oh, cool," he responded just as Preston was about to swoop his camera around for another shot and caught them in his viewfinder. He took a break and cheerfully apologized for interrupting.

"Sorry. I was in the moment."

Making introductions, Todd put his hand on Preston's shoulder and said, "Nick is an old school friend. Nick, this is my boyfriend, Preston."

Ordinarily, the title of boyfriend would have made Preston flinch, but it felt warm and appropriate.

"Great to meet you," Nick smiled. "Isn't it funny how everybody's settling down these days? Maybe it's a post-pandemic thing. I got married last year, and we have a baby on the way."

As Todd exclaimed, "Mazeltov!" Preston asked himself, *Am I settling down?* It was a new sensation but one that was warm in the way the night before with Todd had been.

Preston interviewed Nick for the segment asking, "One wouldn't expect a doctor and family man to be a closet

Titanic fan. What is it about the film that makes you passionate enough to come here today?"

"It's a timeless story," he answered with articulate seriousness. "For all the dramatic elements, it's ultimately a story of hope. As the hero says, 'Make each day count.'"

Preston knew he had his tag line for the segment.

The event was also a remarkable representation of different nationalities, all of whom had made the long journey to be a part of this gathering. There was a 30-year-old Australian collector, Zack, who had spent a literal fortune amassing costumes and props from the film. A fresh-scrubbed young German seamstress named Ilka showed off her obsession with precisely replicating Kate Winslet's costumes, which had led to her highly sought-after couture renditions. Dale, a baby-faced South African artist, made museum-quality miniatures of Titanic characters and set pieces. Some Chinese tween-age girls were running around making film-themed Tik Tok videos.

Plenty of Cameron film nerds were there, too, debating the merits of his other films as compared to *Titanic*. One was even showing off his Na'vi T-shirt from *Avatar*, while his geeky, energetic traveling companion had donned a cap and hoodie with the *Alien* logo and a Ripley action figure duct-taped to his belt.

Almost all attendees knew every line, every frame of the motion picture. Some sported *Titanic* tattoos.

Preston got some sophisticated, analytical grabs from filmmaker Boyd about the power of Titanic to reach across time and demographics to unify people.

"How am I ever going to edit all this good stuff down to three minutes?" he asked Todd.

"You can always make a director's cut," he suggested before adding, "I have to admit, I'm impressed. You might just be turning me into a Titaniac, mister."

Preston asked, "Is it me doing that? Or Milton?"

Todd gave him a peck on the check and simply said, "Same thing."

They wrapped up their successful day of shooting, then took an Uber into downtown Boston so that Preston could thank Todd for all his help and support with a romantic dinner at Mamma Maria's in the city's North End.

"If you ever give up nursing, you could have a brilliant career in TV production," Preston told him as they dove into their delectable meals of clam & crab pasta and black bass.

"I leave the media world to you, thanks."

"Before we head back to Manhattan tomorrow night, I had one more idea to run by you."

Todd put his elbow on the table and leaned in to get as close to him as he could. Smiling, he said, "Bring it on, big guy. I don't think I can say no to you."

"This wouldn't be part of the news segment, it's something strictly personal. Since we're in Boston, maybe we could rent a car in the morning and make a day trip to Springfield."

"Sure. What's there?"

"The cemetery where Milton is buried."

What might have been a morbid little road trip turned out to be a pleasant morning ride of about two hours west from Boston along scenic Route 90. Preston drove the rented Ford Taurus that they'd picked up from Enterprise next to the Holiday Inn Express, while Todd navigated on the GPS. They found a pop station on the radio that was heavy on the Beyonce and Taylor Swift, so they were enjoying cruising along, especially since there was no traffic, and it was a bright and sunny summer day. Nothing on the interstate looked familiar to Milton, but he was pleased that there was still so much lush green foliage in the landscape that was whizzing by.

Todd performed a Google search on Springfield and read the results aloud.

"Notable landmarks in Springfield include the Naismith Memorial Basketball Hall of Fame, commemorating the sport in a striking building."

"Pass."

"Collections at the Springfield Museums include American paintings and sculpture, scientific exhibits, and Asian art. The Amazing World of Dr. Seuss celebrates the beloved children's author. Springfield Armory documents two centuries of military history. The Springfield Cemetery, located in Hampden Country, is also known as the Peabody Cemetery, named for its Unitarian founder, Reverend William Peabody. It contains more than 31,000 burials on 40-plus acres. It includes a Civil War Memorial in the Civil War burial section."

"Milton's body was the 126th recovered in the days after the sinking," Preston told him. "He was returned home, and his parents were eventually buried alongside him. I've seen photos online. Very simple. It's located on Primrose Path East and includes a plaque donated by the Titanic Historical Society. The final sight of land he or any of those killed would have had was when they sailed out of Queenstown, Ireland."

"You leave no stone unturned. Even a headstone. It's nice that the Society remembered him that way."

"Apparently there is another cemetery nearby called Oak Grove where the Society erected a monument to his memory and that of another Springfield resident who died in the sinking, Jane Carr."

"Do you suppose she and Milton know each other?"

"No, they wouldn't have met. Not only was she a third-class passenger, she worked as a domestic and cook. If her body was recovered, it wasn't identified and would likely have been buried at sea."

"The caste system was real. It makes you wonder how many other souls are floating around and not resting in peace."

Milton was struck by this. There had to be others like him, from another time, unseen in these contemporary times waiting for some divine restitution or retribution. Perhaps Jack was among them and, like the book title prophesized, "you were born again to be together."

Guided by the GPS, they made a few turns off the main highway and found themselves at the cemetery's entrance on Maple Street. It resembled a park, with undulating hills and ancient trees lining the paths to the chapel, columbarium, and various burial plots. They parked the Taurus and began to stroll along, looking for Primrose Path. It struck Preston as odd that, in this vast place of interred people from bygone eras, there were no other living mourners to be seen. Todd remained silent and respectful, trying not to think of the eerily reminiscent opening scene from George Romero's classic 1968 horror film *Night of the Living Dead.*

The gardens were beautifully landscaped and well-maintained, creating an aura of serenity. Other than chirping birds and occasional planes passing overhead, all was quiet. It didn't take them long to come upon the Long family plot and the large, square headstone with ornate trim that marked it. It looked to Preston exactly as it had in the online photographs.

It was inscribed with the names "Charles Leonard Long, Harriet Clyde Long, their son Milton Clyde Long" as well as the dates of their births and deaths. The judge had purchased eight plots in total, anticipating that he and Hattie would have been blessed with many children. To lose their only offspring at such a young age was a heartbreak from which they would never recover.

Preston studied the monolith somberly, expectantly waiting for a reaction to ignite from Milton. When none came, Preston silently asked him if it stirred his emotions, but Milton nonchalantly let him know that, *It's just a body down there. I'm quite satisfied with the one I have now.*

Milton's acceptance helped Preston finally understand the meaning behind the grave's inscription, "The seas are quiet, when the winds give o'er; so calm are we when passions are no more."

Chapter Nine

"Fan or Fanatic? Titaniacs Make Each Day Count" may not have been as hard-hitting journalism as some of the other final projects in Professor Grant's class, but it was by far the biggest crowd pleaser, eliciting frequent laughter and even, at times, touching enough to leave a few of Preston's fellow students teary-eyed. After its presentation in the Columbia Auditoria Lecture classroom, there was a generous round of applause that made its creator feel warmly received and accomplished, just as Todd had predicted when they screened it back in his apartment on the laptop.

After two other presentations and when class was dismissed, Wallace Grant asked Preston if he had a few minutes to spare, so, of course, he stayed behind as the others filed out. A few of them gave him their congratulations on the way.

"Great job, Press," his instructor commended with a big smile. "I don't think you'll be surprised with an A grade."

"Better than an A-minus," he kidded.

"I'd've tightened up the editing and made it about thirty seconds shorter, but that's negligible."

"I actually cut together a longer seven minute version which I thought might be fun to try and enter in some short film contests. Assuming there are documentary categories."

"There certainly are. I'd be happy to point you in that direction. That's why I wanted to speak with you."

"That would be cool. And very appreciated," Preston said before Milton added, *Taking this course was a great decision.*

"You have a natural gift."

"Thank you, sir."

Starting to pace as he spoke, Wallace told him, "I think you're too advanced for an internship, but I'd like to recommend you for an entry-level position as an associate producer at my old network's local affiliate here in the city."

"At Channel 7? Really?!"

"It wouldn't pay much to start, but you would get excellent health benefits, a plethora of experience, and meet a wide range of professionals while you further develop your skills. There's no telling where it may lead."

He turned to face Preston and added, "Maybe the sky's the limit."

"Wow. I don't know what to say."

"Say yes," Milton and Wallace told him, simultaneously.

So he did.

"I'll make a call to the news director and give him your email and phone number, if that's all right. You can take it from there."

Preston thought how proud and pleased his parents would be after a decade of his hand-to-mouth, sometimes questionable pursuits as an actor. Milton thought how proud and pleased his parents would be to know his time at Columbia had finally paid off, after all.

Rushing out of the classroom and into the Van Am Quad, Preston immediately fired off a group text to rally the troops for happy hour. He couldn't wait to share the news.

Alanna, Greg, and Marcus were already soon gathered around an outdoor table at Tiki Chick. They'd hardly seen or heard from him since joining what Greg referred to as "the cult of Columbia."

"Big man on campus is finally making time for us again."

"Don't rain on his parade, Greg. Press said he has something big to tell us."

Preston came hurrying up to join them, having race-walked down Amsterdam Avenue from the campus.

"So what's the big announcement?" Alanna asked, as soon as he came into view.

"Todd's on his way. Let's wait for him to get here. I need a drink!"

"We just ordered a pitcher of margaritas," Marcus assured.

"Should we take guesses? A Broadway show?"

"A soap opera?"

"Are you heading to Hollywood?"

"Wrong, wrong, wrong," Preston laughed as the waitress arrived with the pitcher of Margaritas and a Shirley Temple for Alanna.

Greg tried to sound as supportive as he ventured, "Then it must have something to do with your trip to the Titanic convention?"

Grinning slyly, his bestie replied, "Yes and no."

Todd, clad in his scrubs, appeared from around the corner and lit up when he saw Preston with his friends. They gave each other a big, happy kiss on the lips as their friends looked on in anticipation of finally meeting Nurse Charming.

"Todd, these are the friends I've told you about. Alanna, Greg, and Marcus."

"It's great to finally meet you guys."

"Come sit down next to me," Greg said, patting the empty seat beside him. "We've been waiting to check you out."

"You'll have to forgive him," Marcus advised Todd. "He's only in his thirties, but he's already a dirty old man."

As the waitress finished pouring the margaritas, Todd asked, "Do I pass inspection?"

"We all approve," Alanna said, winningly, wishing she could kick Greg under the table, if she could reach him. "Don't we?"

Admiring Todd's impressive biceps, Greg nodded in agreement but couldn't resist adding, "I assume by *all* you're including Milton?"

Preston was in too good a mood to let Greg push his buttons and took Todd's hand in his, saying, "Milton most definitely approves."

"While I appreciate any excuse to meet for happy hour, why have we been so urgently summoned here?" Marcus asked, taking a healthy sip of his frozen tequila concoction.

"Lady and gentlemen, I am happy to inform you that my final project for broadcast journalism class not only garnered applause and an A from the professor…"

"Hey, congrats!"

"That's great, well done, you."

"I knew it," Todd added, giving him another kiss.

"Wait, what else?"

"Wallace is recommending me for a producing position at Channel 7."

Todd nearly tackled him with a bear hug, and the others lifted their glasses in cheers.

Before they could get carried away, Preston qualified that, "I only just found out, so nothing is definite. But if I get a job offer, I've decided to accept it."

"Of course you will," Alanna announced. "Who turns down a TV gig?"

"But what if I'm a one-hit wonder? Can I do more than just a *Titanic* story?"

"Of course you can, baby," Todd promised.

"Instead of going to voice lessons in Murray Hill, I'll probably be holed up in an editing bay somewhere in SoHo."

"Other than Hell's Kitchen, SoHo has the best happy hours in Manhattan," Marcus pointed out. "We would know."

Alanna reached over to give Preston's arm a squeeze and told him, "You're a shoe-in. Proud of you."

"You're not the only one with an announcement, Press," Greg declared.

"Ooh. Are we pregnant?" Marcus teased.

"No, but it's been fun trying. Nonetheless, I have grown fed up waiting for my best friend to make a decision about his birthday that is less than five weeks away, so I have taken matters into my own hands."

"Uh oh," Preston said, sipping his drink.

Speaking with a grandiose air, Greg continued, "Trying to respect Preston's recent personal and....spiritual...enlightenments, I wanted to infuse a maritime motif into the celebrations. Now, Press, you are under no obligation to go along with this, but I needed to get a deposit in before we lose the date. Your birthday is on the final weekend in October before they close for the season."

Everyone assembled looked at Greg expectantly to finish explaining the plan he'd hatched.

"Since it's your thirtieth birthday, I've reserved the main flight deck of the Baylander for thirty people. All aboard starting at five for happy hour."

"On 125th?" Alanna asked, pleased. "I've always wanted to go there. Great idea."

"I thought it was an appropriate nod to Preston's newfound nautical interests."

"It beats the Circle Line," Marcus laughed.

Baylander was a US Navy harbor craft used throughout the Vietnam War before being converted into a helicopter landing pad in 1986. In 2012, it found new life as a lively, floating restaurant docked on the Hudson River at the Harlem Piers utilizing military artifacts as furnishings and decor. The bar and kitchen, serving a wide range of party foods and beverages, were converted from the ship's original storage containers that were utilized to provide meals and supplies for troops in Afghanistan. It was a wildly popular venue with Harlemites, especially in the midsummer months, with views stretching from the George Washington Bridge to the north all the way south to the Chelsea Piers and beyond.

Preston was touched by his friend's thoughtfulness and simply said, "I love it."

In between rounds, Preston excused himself to run to the restroom, and Greg followed after him to seize the chance for a private moment.

"Press, I meant to ask. Should I send Milton an invitation? I don't have his address, but I assume you can get it to him."

After a heavy sigh, Preston dryly said, "Very funny."

Taking his arm to convey his sincerity, Greg told him, "Honey, I have always thought you were a little nuts and that it came with the territory of being an actor. It's one of the multitude of reasons I adore you."

"And…?"

"And if that means I have to love Milton, too, so be it."

※ ※ ※

October 6th was a stunning Sunday in the city with cerulean blue, cloudless skies and mild temperatures that seemed to brighten the mood of everyone who stepped outside. Both of the local baseball teams, the Yankees and the Mets, had won their division playoff games the night before, so even non-sports fans were feeling upbeat in New York. Preston felt the endorphins as soon as he peered through his bedroom curtains to see the morning sunshine begin to pour in. The blast of light caused Todd to stir in bed, and Preston quickly pulled them tightly closed again.

"How is it out there?" Todd asked, groggy.

"Spectacular. Sorry to wake you. Go back to sleep."

Todd squinted at his phone that was on the bed stand, checking the time. It was nearly ten am.

"Nah. It's time to get up."

"It's Sunday. Sleep in some more. We can go for a run or have brunch outdoors somewhere. We won't have days like this in another month. I hope it'll be this nice for my birthday."

Todd propped himself up and Preston admired his rock hard, sculpted torso and thought his boyish, tousled bed head was adorable. It made him want to crawl back into bed and fool around, but before he could, Todd swung his legs out from under the covers and sat up.

"I'll jump in the shower and then get going."

"What's the hurry?" Preston asked. "You're not working today, are you?"

Shaking off his sleepiness, Todd shook his head and told him, "I'm heading to the Park for a rally at eleven."

"A rally? A rally for what?" Preston was curious. Even with a presidential election coming up, he'd never known Todd to express any particular political views.

"To mark one year since the attacks in Israel. One of the families has planned a vigil for the release of the remaining hostages and honor the ones who have died."

Preston felt badly that he hadn't realized it was that somber anniversary, but he was more surprised by the fact that Todd was participating in a commemoration. His surname, Hafkin, was Jewish but Todd had never mentioned anything about his faith.

"You're welcome to come along, but I understand if you don't want to," Todd added, prompting Preston to further appreciate how deftly he always managed to make things easier for anyone in his orbit.

"Sure, I'll go with you. We can get something to eat afterwards."

Todd looked at him sweetly but with an earnest caution. "I expect it to be pretty solemn. A bottomless brunch really wouldn't be an appropriate way to follow it up."

Preston sat beside him and quickly reassured, "If that sounded disrespectful, it wasn't meant to."

Todd gave him a gentle peck on the cheek and said, "There's so much turmoil and division over the situation. This is just a simple way to support the community."

They were quiet for a pensive moment before he added, "I lost two of my cousins who lived in Israel."

"You never told me that, Todd."

"Everyone feels like that have to choose sides over every issue nowadays. I don't want to be put in that position, and I'd never want anyone else to be, either. Especially you."

They moved even closer together and rested their foreheads against each other.

Preston had been raised in the Episcopal church, having been baptized at birth and confirmed after a few childhood years of Sunday school, but that was all perfunctory. He never gave formal religion any thought. He admired Todd's spirituality and ever-present empathy, wanting to be more like him.

Milton spoke to Preston, softly, so as not to interrupt the intimacy of the moment with Todd.

We were a Protestant family and even though we went to church on Christmas and Easter, I don't recall ever praying anywhere else. Not even at the end. I had more faith in Jack than I did in the Lord. What would it hurt to say a prayer?

Preston told Todd, "I'd like to go with you."

"We pray for the protection of those missing among our brethren. Have compassion on them and bring them out from the darkness and the shadow of death. Break their bonds, deliver them from their distress, and bring them swiftly back to their families' embrace. May gladness and joy overtake them and let sorrow flee away. Amen."

Preston watched the African American female rabbi lead the hundreds of people gathered on the lawn just west of the Jackie Onassis Reservoir. There was a large display of hostage photographs that had been named "The Wall of Hope." It was a powerful, moving moment, and he stood quietly beside Todd, who had his head bowed and eyes closed until he eventually responded, "Amen."

A moment of silence followed, but Milton told Preston, *Let's try it.*

Together, Preston and Milton prayed not only for the missing, but for their own families, as well as for Todd and Jack. They asked each other if it had been God who brought them all together. Of course, there was no answer. It seemed as if the only sound were some distant sirens from somewhere outside the Park.

"Let us work together to create a path to peace for all nations," the rabbi concluded, breaking the quietude.

The crowd slowly began to disperse. Preston and Todd ambled past the photo display as they made their way toward one of the walkways leading out of the park and to the street. Preston was reminded of the expanse of passenger photos he's seen with his father at the Titanic exhibition in Philadelphia. More faces of lost loved ones.

The sun was directly overhead and seemed to illuminate the canopy of oak leaves towering over them. Their green hue had just begun to transition to a more muted yellow autumnal shade. The men didn't speak as they strolled, but Todd reached for Preston's hand and clasped it with a warmth that Preston felt was both loving and thankful.

※ ※ ※

Preston was having a lovely dream that he and Todd were walking hand in hand along the deck of a ship, somewhere in the middle of the ocean. The deep waters were calm, and the skies a crystalline blue, without any clouds to obstruct the occasional seagull soaring overhead. No one else was around, if even on board this gliding vessel that cruised along with such grace and ease. Nor was there any land in sight as they floated through the great oceanic expanse like explorers seeing it for the first time.

Todd halted, and Preston stopped too and turned to face him. They brought their lips together. The kiss began gently, and as it built in intensity, so too did the ship's cruising speed. Their passion accelerated along with the nautical power beneath their feet, cutting through the mighty seas with strength and a low, almost indiscernible rumble.

Their lips parted, and the men kissed each other more hungrily until Todd pulled back and cupped Preston's face with his hands.

"Hey there, birthday boy."

Preston opened his eyes and realized he was in his own bed with Todd lying on top of him, holding his face just as he had in the dream. It made him tingle until he shuddered and smiled back, "Good morning."

Preston yielded over to his lover who began thrusting against him. They remained like that for a long time until they finally collapsed in each other's arms, spent and satisfied.

"Thirty is off to a good start," Preston acknowledged.

"Dirty thirty," Todd growled. "Your big day is finally here."

The clock on the nightstand beside Jack's photo read ten ten, and Preston was surprised he'd slept that long.

"Why didn't you wake me sooner?"

"You were sleeping so peacefully, I didn't have the heart."

"I was having the nicest dream. About us. On a cruise."

"I'm glad I woke you before we got to the iceberg."

"No, it wasn't like that at all. It was calm and beautiful."

"I'd've let you sleep longer, but you know how I get in the mornings…"

"Yes, I also know you need to run home and take care of Arnold Palmer before the party."

"Actually, I was woken up by FedEx. They buzzed, but you were out like a light, so I brought in the package. I'm sure it will be the first of many today."

Preston sat up and blinked his sleepy eyes to focus. Sunshine was streaming in through the window, and it looked like a perfect Indian summer day outside.

"May I get it for you?" Todd asked.

Preston nodded and forced himself out of his comfortable, splayed position to sit up while Todd pulled on a pair of boxer shorts and retrieved the delivery. It was a large, poster-sized parcel, elaborately taped up with a combination of bubble wrap, foam, and cardboard.

"Oh, wow," Preston reacted, grabbing his own shorts to wear while he examined the gift and saw the return address. "From my parents."

"Let me get some scissors to get it open."

"On my desk," Preston directed him, curious as to what could be inside. Knowing his parents, it was probably something overly expensive that he'd end up wanting to re-gift.

Getting the outer wrapping off first, a birthday card dropped out, and he opened it to see a traditional Hallmark-style greeting, signed in his mother's handwriting, "May all the years ahead be smooth sailing. We love you." Below that, in his father's hand was written, "Love, Dad and Mom."

Carefully cutting away the remaining protective covering, Preston was able to unveil what was inside, a simple but tastefully matted and framed 12x16 inch print of *R.M.S. Titanic at Sea*, a well known acrylic painting by the distinguished artist Ken Marschall, an icon in the Titanic universe, whose work Preston recognized instantly. It was numbered and signed by Marschall himself.

"That's beautiful," Todd remarked.

"Ken Marschall is almost as famous as Titanic, herself. His work inspired James Cameron so much that he

once said it was his goal to accomplish on film what Ken
had done on canvas."

"You'll have to find a place of honor for it," Todd
suggested.

"It's great. I'll call and thank them. Super
thoughtful."

Todd began picking up the rest of his clothes, saying,
"I'll get going, but call me when you know what time you
want me to pick you up to head to Baylander. And I know
it's October, but wear sunscreen, please."

"Aye Aye, nurse."

Watching Todd zip up his jeans and slip on his
sweater made Preston feel a bit guilty. The poor guy was
always running to and from meeting him.

"Todd, you know it's not like I'm allergic to cats or
anything. I could stay at your place, once in a while."

"Anytime. I'm flexible."

"Yes, you are," he quipped flirtatiously before
standing up and moving intimately close to him. "Maybe it's
time we think about consolidating our living arrangements."

"Mister Spaulding, is that a proposition?"

"Let's call it a consideration."

"I shall take that under advisement," he said, bestowing another kiss on his partner before heading out the door.

Preston walked into the adjacent bathroom, pausing to take a look at himself in the medicine chest mirror, evaluating his image at thirty years of age. Dissolving into view beside his reflection was Milton's face, wearing a light smile.

Happy Birthday, old man, Milton greeted.

"Happy Birthday to you, sir!" he said back, happy to see him. "It's been a while. Where have you been?"

I've been watching. I didn't want to distract you when you've been so busy with your new job. It seems like you're making quite a success of yourself.

"I'm loving it. Every day they give me more responsibility. Couldn't have gotten there without you, Milton."

You could have, but maybe you wouldn't have. I'm glad it's going so well with Todd, too. He is a good man.

"Yes, he is. Thank you for pointing me in the right direction."

We've been teaching each other.

"I consider you a friend. Is that weird?"

Milton shook his head and said, *We're more than friends, Chuckaboo. We're kindred spirits.*

Chapter Ten

Milton was pleased with the positive changes in Preston's life and felt he had earned the celebration that was in store for him aboard the Baylander. It prompted Milton to recall the last birthday gift he had ever received from his parents, the extravagant Swiss winter holiday to St. Moritz, bestowed with the strict caveat from his mother that he would not attempt a toboggan ride on the famed Cresta Run. Even with training and practice rides, racing headfirst down the natural ice track at speeds up to eighty miles per hour was a risk Harriet Long would not allow her son to take.

His own death certificate stated his profession as a "gentleman of leisure," and since he had abandoned his scholarly pursuits at Columbia—to his parents' lasting puzzlement—that had indeed become a full-time occupation for him, streaking from one lavish vacation to the next. While it undoubtedly made for a glamorous lifestyle, it was ultimately unfulfilling. Milton had never been able to surmise whether he was running to or from something.

In his handsome suite at the famed and luxurious Badrutt Palace Hotel, Milton was among the many international wealthy elite who lodged there to enjoy fashionable seasonal activities such as ice skating, skiing, curling, sleigh rides, and hikes. The chateau-themed resort was romantic, not only in its design but in the indulgent way the Badrutt family pampered their clientele. It reminded Milton of the mansion Castra Regis in Bram Stoker's *The Lair of the White Worm*, the popular book he had just finished reading on his voyage from the United States.

A group of young tourists from London's Belgravia neighborhood arrived at the same time and made themselves well-known to other hotel guests and staff from the moment they burst into the well-appointed lobby. They were a boisterous octet of five men and three women, friends with too much money and too little responsibility, who had come to the Badrutt to frolic and cavort. Milton observed them with a mixture of both distaste and envy, finding their rambunctious public behavior in the fancy environs of St. Moritz to be gauche, yet still he somehow longed to be a part of their fun-loving clique. It seemed as if their loud peals of nonstop laughter echoed everywhere on the property, impossible to avoid or ignore.

Milton thought they all looked like typical affluent young people, the men decked out in their custom-tailored suits and the ladies in bespoke, fashionable dresses accessorized by ornate, expensive jewelry. Their energy and enthusiasm for the holiday was evident as they merrily careened from one activity to another, with stops in the hotel dining room, ski lodge, and the Renaissance Bar with its enormous open fireplace and sweeping view of the Alps. It was a venue described as a sanctuary, but when the band of revelers was there, it was certainly not the case.

As he began to see them wherever he went, Milton thought one member of their party stood out from the others: a striking-looking, swarthy young man with an obviously solid but lithe physique. Possessing an unusually dark complexion, chocolate-brown eyes and curly, almost-black hair, he had an exotic look that could have been brooding or even menacing if he weren't perpetually flashing a bright smile that showed off defined dimples and a chiseled jawline. Milton tried unsuccessfully not to stare.

One morning, Milton hadn't been inclined to have breakfast and instead found himself taking coffee in the lobby and thumbing through their collection of magazines. One of the European periodicals were filled with articles blatantly soliciting America to join in a war against the looming threats from Germany, something that President Taft opposed in favor of a pacifist position. Preferring a pleasant distraction over politics, Milton spent more time with *National Geographic,* which included a seventeen-page foldout panorama of the Canadian Rockies.

He was struggling to refold the paper back into place just as the merrymakers were sweeping through on their way out of the hotel. He looked up to see the attractive, ever-smiling dark one coming closer, and they noticed each other for long enough to motivate the young man to offer Milton a friendly wave before calling out, "Ciao, ragazzo!"

So, he was Italian. That explained his looks, even though he'd overheard him speaking perfect English with his cohorts. Shyly, Milton courteously waved in return.

"I'll meet you outside," he called to his friends as he held back to look directly at Milton, whose heart was suddenly in his throat because of the impromptu social exchange. He straightened up from his more relaxed position in the lobby armchair.

"We're off to go skating," he said to Milton with an English accent tinged only slightly with an Italian flair. "Care to meet us there?"

Taken completely off guard, Milton managed to stammer a response. "Thank you, but I have some reading to do this morning." He internally chastised himself for such a pitiful excuse, especially when he was holding one of the hotel's magazines in his lap.

"If you change your mind, you'll know where to find us," the fellow cheerfully said before adding, "I am Sebastian."

"Milton Long, how do you do?"

"Cheerio, Milton," the carefree Sebastian replied before turning and hurrying off to rejoin his friends.

They were all so young, outgoing, and self-assured, Milton thought. Sebastian, especially. Of course, Milton told himself, he too could be just as confident if he had that much personality and beauty. And unlike himself, Milton assumed Sebastian was probably a terrific ice skater.

The next time he saw the band of Brits was in the late afternoon at the Badrutt Salon, where he was enjoying a light repast of consommé and tea. They bustled past his table on the way to their own, seeming to all talk over each other about the events of their day's activities.

Sebastian noticed him and again encouraged him to join them. "Milton. Have you been inside the hotel all day? Come have a drink with us. We need to warm up." Two of the young ladies in the group noticed and chimed in with similar congeniality.

"Yes, please do."

"Don't be by yourself."

Carefully, Milton put down his napkin and rose to accompany them over to their large table by the window, overlooking another spectacular Alpine vista. Sebastian gave him a hearty, approving pat on the back that made him feel warmly welcomed. More than wishful thinking, he couldn't help but imagine it somehow meant more than camaraderie. Now up close to Sebastian, Milton could see how very young he was—perhaps barely twenty.

"We expect you to live up to the American reputation for adventure, Yankee Doodle," Sebastian laughed, pulling out a chair next to his own seat for Milton to occupy.

One of the others ordered Pommeau for the table, a fortified cider aged in oak barrels that was a popular aperitif. As introductions were made around the table, Milton sipped the beverage and savored its notes of caramel and honey, which seemed to intermingle perfectly with the scent of cardamom cologne he could detect on his new acquaintance.

Sebastian, he learned, was another well-off dilettante, thanks to his very wealthy Briton father, a high-level executive at J.P. Morgan's International Mercantile Company, who had met Sebastian's Venetian mother while on a business tour of Italy.

"That explains his complexion and luxurious locks," one of the women, Emily, teased.

"Like Michelangelo's *David*, but better dressed," another, named Louise, added with a mock-scandalous tone.

"All right, that's enough of that talk," one of their laddish friends called Bruce interjected. "You're bordering on buggery!"

Everyone laughed and Milton forced a chuckle to fit in with their levity.

Sebastian leaned over to Milton and, with self-deprecating humor, told him, "You see, I'm a half-breed. Accepted, but not respected."

"What about you, Milton? What do you do back in the States?" Emily asked, although she didn't seem genuinely interested.

"He's a bookworm, I know that much," Sebastian chimed in.

"I'm on sabbatical from my studies at Columbia University," he fibbed with his natural smirk, telling himself that it was a partial truth.

"Oh? What field?"

"My father is a judge," he answered, playing for time until he concocted an answer. "So…law."

"Aren't you getting too old to be a schoolboy?" Bruce quizzed. "What are you, twenty-three or -four?"

Trying not to blush, Milton defensively lied, "Twenty-two."

"I simply detested school," Louise said in a sing-song voice. "I decided my time would be better spent traveling before I have to settle down and start a family."

"Skiing tomorrow?" another one of them asked to change the subject. "Looks to be perfect weather for it."

"What about the Cresta?" Sebastian suggested, making Milton tense up.

"You're on your own for that," Emily said, waving him off. "One of the maids told me that someone shattered his clavicle just yesterday."

Milton was relieved but also strangely annoyed that his mother, as usual, had been proven right. "Mother knows best" was one of her favorite expressions.

"Skiing it is, then," Sebastian proclaimed with authority.

It was a pleasant day for them on the slopes of Corviglia with quality equipment from the Badrutt's ski shop available to rent prior to taking the cable car to the top of the resort's nearby mountain. Milton admitted that he was still a novice when it came to the sport, and Sebastian assured him that there were trails for all skill levels.

The pristine, cloudless blue skies accentuated the cold but windless air. Milton loved the bracing 26-degree temperature and didn't shiver in the least, feeling keenly alive—especially alongside Sebastian, who had a knack for keeping the coterie entertained. Everyone except Bruce stayed with the Intermediate runs and the hours flew by until they were all exhausted. At one point, Milton took a minor tumble on his way down, and it seemed as if Sebastian appeared out of nowhere to check on him.

"You okay, boy?" he asked with his ever-present smile, simultaneously offering Milton a hand to help him back up.

Flushed as his gloved hand took Sebastian's for support, Milton hoisted himself upright and smiled back, "Thank you, I'm wonderful."

Worn out by the late afternoon, everyone agreed to return to the hotel for a rest before dinner. Carriages waited at the bottom of the slopes to shuttle guests back to the Badrutt. Milton instinctively lingered behind, still uncertain how accepted he'd been received by the clique. Sebastian noticed and kept up with his natural inclination to look out for others, so remained alongside his new friend.

"Tomorrow, we should try cross country," Bruce enthused.

"I suspect my legs will be too sore for anything but a Turkish bath," Emily countered.

"That sounds heavenly," Louise agreed.

They began to climb into a carriage, but it was fully occupied before Milton and Sebastian could join them.

"Go ahead, we will get in the next one," Sebastian told them cheerfully, closing the carriage door.

Milton was breathless at the thought of getting to spend some time alone with the dashing young man and wondered if it was an intentional ploy on his part.

"Sorry about that," Milton practically stammered. "You could have squeezed in if it weren't for me."

"It's nice to have a break from them," he said sotto voce, feigning a conspiratorial tone. "I say, why don't we take a sleigh ride back, instead? My treat. They'll be green with envy."

Such a luxury, gliding through a snow-covered forest or across a frozen lake in a horse-drawn, open-air sleigh, was considered one of the most romantic experiences available to tourists. Snugly tucked under fur blankets while riding across exquisitely picturesque terrains would certainly be attractive for honeymoon couples, not two young bachelors, but Sebastian didn't seem in the least concerned about societal appearances.

"I'm game if you are," Milton told him, covering his intense delight at the prospect.

Sebastian stepped momentarily away to request the service from one of the nearby carriage-men. Milton noticed him handing over some currency to the happily obliging worker.

Rejoining Milton, Sebastian grinned, "It won't be a minute. They'll have one for us straight away."

In no time at all, as the sun began to dip behind the mountainscape, two beautiful brown draft horses rounded the corner, pulling a brightly painted green carriage with shiny, polished steel blades and traditional jingling bells. It was small and built for two passengers. The horses clopped slowly along, driven by a portly, red-faced older gentleman in a top hat and bundled up in a heavy black coat, with a plaid woolen blanket draped across his lap.

The driver was Italian, as was much of the working class there, due to its geographical proximity to Italy. He and Sebastian spoke in that language.

As the men hauled themselves into the wool-lined seats behind the driver, Sebastian explained, "I told him we

are bound for the hotel, but to take his time and show us
some of the sights. This will be a lark!"

They spread the fur blankets across themselves and
settled into their seats. Because of the compact size of this
particular sleigh, they found themselves pressed against each
other, knee to knee. Milton's physical proximity to
Sebastian was titillating, and he found himself suddenly
happier and more aroused than he could remember being in
a long time. Perhaps ever.

The tranquil scenery of the snowy, primeval forest
was beautiful to behold, and they rode along in silence,
admiring the views. The only sound they could hear was the
footfall of the horses' hooves harmonizing with the ringing
bells and the whoosh of the snow as they plowed forward.
The driver urged his charges faster, and the rush of the wind
hit their faces, making them laugh with intoxicating delight.

At a brisk trot, the horses propelled the sleigh
quickly out of the forest and back onto the main trail
heading through the village of St. Moritz. It was a heady
moment, and Milton had finally managed to let go of his
inhibitions, as if they had flown off and were left behind in
the dense mountain woods.

They rounded a significant curve, and, at such an
elevated speed, Sebastian was thrown right up against

Milton, and they both guffawed at the lively whirlwind experience.

"Sorry about that," he shouted to Milton as the sleigh continued to careen along.

"I'm not," Milton answered, but Sebastian couldn't hear him. As they resumed their riding positions, Milton's gloved hand reached for Sebastian's upper leg, underneath the warm bear fur. It came to rest on his thigh and Milton couldn't resist squeezing it with affection and appreciation.

Sebastian's head jerked over to face Milton, with an open-mouthed expression of shocked indignation. Simultaneously, he roughly shoved Milton's hand off him, and, for a brief moment, Milton thought he was about to be struck.

Milton wanted to immediately apologize but was too wounded to speak. This must be what it felt like to be shot, he thought.

"Sei pazzo?" Sebastian yelled. Milton had no clue what that meant, but it couldn't be good.

The sleigh settled back into a slower rhythm as it continued on a straight path forward, but the pleasure in their joy ride had been eradicated in a flash.

"I am not that way, Milton," he said firmly, conscientious to maintain some privacy from the driver lest he speak better English that he let on. "I did not mean to give you the impression that…" He was searching for the right words before cruelly settling on, "…that I am like you."

Milton turned away and felt his stomach turn and his lower lip tremble. He held his breath in a reflexive way to fight the onset of tears ready to well up in his eyes.

They rode in awkward silence back to the hotel, where they dismounted from the sleigh, both refusing assistance from the driver. Milton walked a few paces behind Sebastian as they entered the lobby, and, before they parted, Sebastian paused and spoke without looking him in the eye. "Good night, sir. I think it best that you return to conducting your own holiday from here on."

Devastated and mortified, Milton could only nod and managed to croak out, "Good night."

There was no more contact between Milton and the others for the remainder of his time in St. Moritz, although they exchanged polite waves and nods when seeing each other in occasional passing. Every time brought back his feelings of shame and embarrassment. Milton consulted with the Badrutt concierge about shortening his stay, saying that the cold temperatures were playing havoc on his sinuses and that he wanted to pivot to Marseille or Nice before having to return to Southampton for his eventual voyage back to America.

When he checked out the next morning, the gentleman working at the desk told Milton there was a small package that had been left for him and handed him a parcel wrapped in brown paper, tied with a string. When he finally had settled into his seat for the long train ride to Marseilles, Milton opened and discovered two brand new, popular books, *Peter Pan* and *Ethan Frome*.

A plain card was tucked into the front cover of one, and Milton pulled out to read what had been neatly written by the hand that just yesterday he had longed to hold, but then had nearly hit him.

"I'll never get to reading these, but I wish that you will enjoy them. They will keep you company on your future travels. Sebastian."

※※※

Even without any discernible current on the Hudson River, the Baylander was rocking literally and figuratively. For its final weekend of the season, every available deck of the ship was packed with revelers, and the DJ's upbeat dance music made the atmosphere feel as festive as a public holiday weekend.

Preston's thirty guests occupied the Main Flight Deck, where twinkling lights and paper lanterns were strung overhead and mylar balloons, including a pair shaped like "3-0," tied around the railings. Picnic tables were decorated with matching placemats, napkins, and streamers as waiters brought out seemingly never ending servings of lobster rolls, fried calamari, tacos, and burgers.

Greg, already well lubricated before the festivities even began, stumbled over to the rail where his bestie was chatting with Todd and Alanna. Marcus dutifully followed behind, keeping an eye on his wobbly partner. Greg handed Preston a double Captain's Colada and encouraged him to drink up.

"You have some catching up to do, Press," he slurred, trying to hold his phone steadily enough to take some selfies.

"It's a marathon, not a sprint," he laughed.

"A reminder that I have enacted a strict no-politics policy," Greg reminded them, with authority. "There will be zero discussion of the Presidential election at this gathering. I won't have our fun ruined."

"Smart move," Marcus concurred. "Although it's no secret which side of the fence you're on."

"You'd better be on my side, too, gurl. My side is the right side."

Marcus bantered back, "No, baby, you're way on the Left side."

Over Marcus's shoulder, Greg was scanning the deck which was becoming more crowded with guests. "I don't even know half of these people," he confided to them in a not-so-soft whisper. "Who are they?"

"Some of Todd's friends I've acquired, some classmates from Columbia, and a bunch of my new coworkers from Channel 7."

Greg gasped, "Is the sexy weatherman here? The one with the bubble butt?"

"Sorry, pal. The behind-the-scenes team, only."

Marcus interjected, "They let you report on the air sometimes. We've seen all your stories. You're great on whatever side of the camera you're working on."

"What about Milton?" Greg asked, looking up to the sky. "Is he…you know, around?"

Todd cut in with, "I've learned that Milton is never far away."

A new guest was arriving, walking up the gangway, and Alanna noticed the classy, trim brunette, arriving solo.

"Who dat?" she asked.

Preston's eyes widened as he instantly recognized the young woman and excused himself to greet her.

"You are L.A., are you not?" he asked with his arms open, awaiting confirmation before embracing her.

"I am. Milton, I presume?"

They simultaneously laughed and moved into a warm, happy hug.

Lesley-Anne "L.A." Beadles, Ph.D., was a distinguished historian from North Carolina who'd risen to viral fame with history lovers, especially those interested in all things Titanic. Preston had been a fan since he discovered her "Unsinkable" podcast and her proud "obsession with the micro and macro of Titanic, with every person who boarded her in 1912." In addition to that cataclysmic event, she also had a specialization in the history of the US South and an esteemed project entitled "Mythic Americana" that examined the way culture mythologizes its own past.

Preston had initially reached out to her online, ostensibly to arrange a research interview with her for a TV story he was working on about the upcoming restoration of Grant's Tomb in nearby Morningside Heights. That led to a phone call during which they discovered each other's vivacious personalities and immediately hit it off.

"I read on Wikipedia that one million people turned out for the dedication," Preston marveled during their conversation. "With more than 50,000 in the parade march. That's a lot of people for 1897. It's hard to imagine drawing a crowd like that nowadays."

"Back then, people weren't distracted by other events or the internet. And he was a national hero," she explained with an affable expertise that was still relatable to the non-historical layman. "Ulysses was on the right side of history, even if he didn't know it then. The right man for the moment, so it was a big deal to honor him in such a grand manner."

She went on to comment that the way time had rewritten the narrative of the Civil War was a romanticization of the Old South, as evidenced in works such as *Gone with the Wind.*

The conversation, not too surprisingly, segued to the subject of Titanic when he observed that the same could be said of her tragic end; how a global catastrophe was now predominantly remembered as a "soap opera at sea" that glossed over the thousands of real men and women affected by its loss.

"Not to mention how it rattled civilization's faith in technology and the existing societal class and gender norms," she added. "It was also the beginning of the end for the Edwardian Era and its established hierarchy."

He consequently shared the basic gist of his association with Milton Long, cautious not to get too much into the otherworldly aspect of it, lest he jeopardize having a potential new colleague and friend. She had turned out to be delightfully receptive and promised they would meet the next time she was in New York City.

As it happened, she had arrived in town the day before to attend a symposium at Fordham University, and Preston had invited her to come to the party and celebrate his and Milton's, thirtieth birthdays.

Taking in the jolly scene, she told him, "I think this is a spectacular way to honor his memory. I also have an actress friend here in town I want to introduce you to. She's auditioning for the revival of the musical *Titanic* and has written herself a monologue from the point of view of the Countess of Rothes. Since you're an actor yourself, I thought she'd benefit from your perspective."

Titanic the stage musical was a 1997 Tony Award winner that would soon be heading back to Broadway in a new production. Theater lovers, even those not prone to attending Titanic conventions, were already clamoring for advanced ticket purchases. The ship may have foundered, but the ongoing public interest in Titanic was as evergreen and in-demand as Mickey Mouse or Coca Cola.

Wallace Grant and his wife were making their way up to board the ship not far behind L.A. and Preston noticed them over her shoulder. He'd invited his professor-turned-mentor, but hadn't expected him to show up.

"L.A., you're going to love this guy. You're two of the smartest people I know."

And so it went for the next two hours as everyone mingled merrily, danced, ate, and drank, until finally a giant sheet cake, plainly but expertly decorated with icing that read "Happy 30th, Preston," was presented, adorned with thirty candles. Greg was circling around like a vulture, capturing the moment in photos and videos, promising to tag people on social media.

After everyone assembled, including a few others from adjacent decks, they sang "Happy Birthday" to Preston, and he surprised himself by being able to extinguish all the candles in only two breaths, wondering if Milton was somehow helping. He hoped so.

In the cab ride back to Preston's apartment, he was sitting knee to knee with Todd, already happily recounting the party's happiest and most memorable moments.

Todd advised, "You know, I haven't given you *my* present yet."

"Aww, you sweet man. You're my greatest present every day."

"You don't want it then?"

"I didn't say that! What is it? Where is it?"

Todd reached into the breast pocket of his blazer and pulled out an envelope. He handed it to Preston, who opened it. It was too dark to see properly, so Todd switched on his phone light for him.

It was a travel itinerary. Two First-Class tickets from New York to Cork, Ireland, with one short layover at London's Heathrow Airport. From Cork Airport, it was a short drive to the quaint port town of Cobh, formerly known as Queenstown. This had been Titanic's final stop on her maiden voyage before she headed out to sea and met her fate. It was the last sight of land for anyone on board who would perish, and the destination had become an off-the-beaten-path mecca for Titanic enthusiasts, as opposed to the more high-profile mega-museum in Northern Ireland that had almost completely repurposed Belfast.

"I didn't want that Holiday Inn Express in Boston to be our only holiday together," Todd said, lovingly.

"I'm all for making new memories with you," Preston agreed. "I'll have to see about getting time off from my job, though."

"I already thought of that. Look at the dates."

He had organized for them to arrive in Cobh on April 11, the same day as in 1912 when Titanic sailed from there.

"See? I can use Google, too," Todd kidded. "It's not too ghoulish, is it?"

"No way, it's perfect. I love it."

Preston bent forward to gently rest his forehead against Todd's. He wasn't the least bit uncertain when he added, "I love you, too."

Chapter Eleven

Always keen to capitalize on any opportunity to further his burgeoning TV career, Preston not only put in for April vacation time to make the trip to Ireland, he also pitched "The Titanic Trail" as a special travel segment at the next story meeting he had with the newsroom brass, offering to shoot highlights on his iPhone to bring home for editing. Liked not only for his personality, but also for his work ethic, Preston won them over to the idea if he could promise to make it accessible to the average viewer.

Unaware of his intimate connection to the Titanic tale, they just assumed he was a clever brainstormer when he immediately proposed tying it in as an offbeat tourist destination for history buffs, once they exhausted the significant Titanic-related sites right there in NYC.

Preston expertly rattled off a list of locations that left his colleagues wide-eyed and impressed. From the Upper West Side's Straus Memorial Park, to the plaques commemorating Ida and Isidor inside Macy's Department Store, there were many other important local spots to exploit.

True to the reputation he was quickly acquiring, he presented a detailed inventory for their review and consideration. At Chelsea Piers, there were the ghostly remnants of the White Star Line piers where Titanic had been set to arrive but instead welcomed the Carpathia carrying its only survivors. The nearby Jane Hotel had once been the American Seaman's Friend Society Sailor's Home, where lodging and food were provided for many of the crew members and passengers after they disembarked from the Carpathia. Located in the South Street Seaport, the Titanic Memorial Lighthouse was dedicated the year after the sinking, financed by public donations.

He also read a breakdown of several other markers around the City, honoring passengers who perished. "Twenty-five-year-old first-class passenger Edith Corse Evans is remembered by an inscribed stained glass window inside Broadway's Grace Church. Another first-class victim was William T. Stead who, after helping others into lifeboats, awaited his demise inside the smoking room. A modest profile depiction of his bearded face adorns a 5th Avenue wall on the Upper East Side."

"How did you come up with all this?" one of the producers asked, her eyebrows raised in amazement.

"I've always liked homework," he grinned and continued on, showing off for his impressed audience. "Arguably Titanic's most famous passenger and one of the world's richest men, John Jacob Astor IV, was buried inside Washington Heights' Trinity Church, as well as, immortalized by a stained glass window in the Cathedral of St. John the Divine. Another multimillionaire fatality was Benjamin Guggenheim, who famously changed into his finest tuxedo, 'prepared to go down like a gentleman.' His family's namesake art museum, The Guggenheim, is of course world renowned and a fixture of New York City culture."

"I had no idea about any of this," someone else remarked.

Preston read on from his notes. "There are landmarks for some who made it back to dry land, as well. Henry Harris may have died, but his widow Irene came back to take over the management of the Hudson Theater he founded and became the first female theatrical producer on Broadway. One of the great heroes of the Titanic story was Colonel Archibald Gracie, who miraculously managed to await the Carpathia's arrival while clamoring onto an overturned lifeboat. He went on to write one of the most personal accounts of the disaster before he perished eight months later. His simple headstone in the Bronx's Woodlawn Cemetery reads 'Hero of the Titanic.'"

"Okay, Okay, Press," the news director chuckled, holding up his hands in mock surrender. "We're sold."

The professional green light only added to Preston's excitement about the trip with Todd, and it became their main topic of conversation when they were together, increasingly at Todd's West Village apartment where Preston was trying to get used to what it was like having a cat in the house. If they were going to eventually live together, it would be a necessary adjustment—just like whether to leave the toilet lid up or if used coffee mugs go in the sink or in the dishwasher.

Felines notoriously had minds of their own, and this one was not an exception.

Arnold Palmer was a jet black, indoors-only five-year-old cat that Todd had rescued shortly after moving to Manhattan, having found him abandoned in Central Park. He was a malnourished, flea-bitten kitten someone had left there inside a soggy shoebox. When he told Preston Arnie's origin story, he couldn't help but think that his sweet partner was always a dedicated caregiver, even outside of work hours.

The sight of Arnie's litter box in the bathroom took some getting used to for Preston, especially when the feline used his paw to intrude on whoever was in there when it was time to do his business. Fortunately, Todd was fastidiously clean.

The cat also had a knack for being everywhere the men were, following them from room to room and curling himself alongside them, even in bed.

Preston didn't resist being charmed by the constant nuzzling and started to understand the appeal for "cat people." Naturally, this led to his curiosity about further Titanic connections related to house pets.

Preston had already read about the dozen dogs who were on board Titanic, three of which were able to survive because of their diminutive size; kept in their owners' staterooms instead of the ship's kennel located near Titanic's fourth, dummy funnel. Arnie stimulated his interest in finding out about any felines that may have been aboard, and Preston was quite delighted to discover and tell Todd the story of Jenny.

"Jenny was a 'mouser' who initially lived aboard Titanic's sister ship in Belfast, the Olympic. She was allowed to freely roam the decks to help control the rat population and was cared for by an Irish stoker named Jospeh Mulholland. One legend claimed that Jenny gave birth to a litter of kittens on board Titanic before they sailed from Southampton and was seen carrying her newborns, one by one, off to dry land. This was considered by some, especially Mulholland, to be an ominous omen of the voyage to come. He himself disembarked at Southampton, now having 'an uneasy feeling about the ship.' In saving herself and her offspring, Jenny was also credited with saving the stoker."

"Maybe part of Jenny lives on in Arnie," Todd mused, playing along and hoping that such a fanciful hypothesis might help further endear his pet to his boyfriend.

It seemed to work because it was Preston who brought up the subject of who would cat-sit for Arnold Palmer while they were on their trip, and Todd assured him that one of his friendly neighbors had already volunteered.

Preston's new passions crept into his conversations with his parents, too, and instead of dreading or putting off their calls, he found himself looking forward to telling them about his new reporting assignments, his times out in the City with Todd and, of course, anticipation for the upcoming European trip.

"I insist on sending you a check to buy yourself some decent luggage at Bloomingdales," Liz told him. "You can't keep slinging around a duffle bag like you're a backpacker!"

Meanwhile, Brandon was now regularly and enthusiastically emailing him newsletters and announcements for cultural exhibits and events he felt Preston would find of interest for possible news stories.

"Now that you've turned into a history buff, I think you'll really find some of these useful. And I know it's daunting, but I highly recommend you read *The Power Broker*. Every New Yorker should know more about Robert Moses."

Preston was most touched to hear his father end a phone call with, "When you're back from Ireland, you really need to bring Todd down for a visit, so we can finally meet him." It was an all-new level of communication for them.

Milton agreed and told Preston not to worry about anything and simply relax and enjoy his special holiday with his wonderfully attentive and generous partner.

On the April morning of their departure, Todd arrived at Preston's place so they could get a ride share together to the airport.

"Come on in the bedroom. A little last minute packing, but I'm almost ready."

Todd watched from the doorway as Preston zipped up the last of his toiletries into a Dopp kit before it went into

the suitcase. As usual, he noticed the framed image of Jack
Thayer looking on from the bookshelf. He'd come to accept
the idea of Milton being a part of their relationship, but he
felt strangely jealous of the other long-dead stranger who
had such a prominent place in their lives.

Even so, Todd couldn't resist asking mock-casually,
"If we eventually *do* move in together, is he coming with
us?

"He, who?" asked Preston, looking up from his
newly purchased luggage. He then noticed Todd's eyes
directed at the picture of Jack and realized.

Preston's head tilted empathically. He smiled and
moved to the shelf, proceeding to place the frame, face
down.

"I'll make sure to take a nice one of you in Ireland
and replace it when we get back." Preston then walked to his
steadfast lover and wrapped his arms around his torso before
planting an intense, meaningful kiss squarely on his lips.

※※※

It was April 10, five days before the anniversary that
always boosted Irish tourism almost as much as St. Patrick's

Day. Even with an hour's delay while the airline dealt with a mechanical maintenance issue, they arrived at London's Heathrow Airport in plenty of time to transfer to their connecting flight to Cork which was, by comparison, a short hop of only ninety minutes. Preston spent much of the time taking in the aerial view from his window seat, thinking Milton would appreciate his first experience flying in a plane.

Once back on the ground, they were soon in the back of a rather beat-up old taxi that drove them a further half hour out of the cosmopolitan city center to the small port town of Cobh. It was easy to be charmed by the sights of the fertile farmlands, lush countryside, and dramatic skies. Ireland was already enchanting.

Located on the south side of the Great Island in Cork Harbour, Cobh was the home to Ireland's only dedicated cruise terminal and resembled a fairy tale illustration with its Gothic Cathedral, St. Colman's, dominating the skyline overlooking the water and multicolored buildings that had been there since the early twentieth century.

Reading through his travel and tourism brochures, Todd pointed out that multiple outlets declared Cobh one of the most beautiful small towns in Europe. Preston imagined that it all still looked pretty much as Milton would have seen it in 1912.

The grizzled driver, Padrick, who resembled a character straight out of *Finian's Rainbow,* gave them a bit more insight into the local history as he spoke to them in a thick brogue, "'Tis a far cry from when it was named Queenstown and known as the saddest place on earth. Over the course of a century, more than two and a half million Irish emigrants sailed from here to flee poverty and famine. On the brighter side, 'tis also the home of the world's first ever yacht club, founded in 1720."

"We'll be walking the Titanic Trail tomorrow," Preston told him.

"You'll find it very interesting," Padrick replied, adding, "but you know there's also a connection to another tragedy at sea here in Cobh. Three years after Titanic was lost, the Lusitania was torpedoed by German U-boats off the old head of Kinsale about an hour's drive south of your hotel. Nearly 1200 people drowned, and many of them are buried in Cobh's Old Churchyard."

Still more lost souls, Preston thought to himself.

The car wound its way down to Westbourne Place in the town center and stopped in front of the handsome looking Commodore Hotel—a large structure painted a pastel blue sandwiched between two other buildings in complementary shades of peach and yellow. Lined up on the hillside were rows of colorfully painted houses nicknamed "the Deck of Cards." They overlooked a modern looking park adorned with pavilions. Flag- and flower-draped walking paths were adjacent to the expansive and scenic harbor.

Looking out at the placid water, the sun setting as a few sailboats glided along in the gentle April early evening breeze, Preston realized he had been inadvertently holding his breath. With a big exhale, he said, "We made it."

Todd wondered if Preston was talking to him or to Milton.

The hotel was fully booked as was customary in April, the anniversary of Titanic's sailing from Cobh Harbour. It was only thanks to Todd's thoughtfulness and pre-planning that they were able to have secured their modest accommodations in a King Sea View suite. Once they checked in and found their room, Preston and Todd sat side by side on the bed facing the windows with a panoramic view of the Harbour. Night had fallen, and the only outside illumination came from the street lamps and a few twinkling lights from boats still on the water. The temperature had dropped noticeably, and it seemed as if a fog on the horizon was visibly moving closer inland.

It was on this very day, 113 years earlier, that one hundred twenty three people had also arrived by train in then-Queenstown and found their night's accommodation in the quaint, tiny town. Some of them lodged at the Commodore, known at the time as the Queens Hotel in honor of Queen Victoria, who had first set foot in Ireland only a few steps away. The next morning they would board what they perceived as the world's mightiest and most beautiful vessel, RMS Titanic. If one of those passengers had stayed in this same room, the hotel didn't advertise it, and neither Preston nor Milton felt any particular close spiritual connection in its atmosphere.

Their silent reverie was interrupted by a surprisingly loud growl from Todd's stomach, and they both burst into laughter.

"Someone's hungry," Preston said.

"It's been a long time since lunch," Todd chuckled. He had done all the homework for their voyage and suggested, "There's a place called The Titanic Bar and Grill around the corner. Shall we go grab a bite?"

"I suspect we'll get our fill of themed content tomorrow on the Titanic Trail, but you're incredibly sweet to suggest it. Why don't we just go to the bistro downstairs?"

Served by a friendly redheaded lass named Eve, they enjoyed a hearty meal of tasty fish and chips, washed down with Guinness stouts in keeping with their Irish theme. Todd liked the beer better than Preston who switched over to a vodka and soda, leaving Todd to finish the rest of his beer.

I never cared for it, either, Milton mentioned.

Eve asked which of the many tour packages they had selected for the next day, and she told them how much they would enjoy meeting its founder and guide, Dr. Michael Martin, who was a retired Naval officer and charismatic historian.

"You must be knackered from your travels," she observed. "You'll want to rest up tonight, lads. Dr. Martin will be walking your feet off in the morning."

Soon after, when they finally climbed into their comfortable bed fully intending to make love in this faraway new land, they both fell immediately into a deep, restful sleep.

The next morning, after a light continental breakfast in their room, Preston and Todd emerged from the hotel to meet Dr. Martin just outside the lobby entry where the tour would begin. They wore light windbreaker jackets, and

Todd brought along a small collapsible umbrella in case there was a rain shower. It was a mild, overcast morning, which Preston thought was appropriately somber given the anniversary they were marking; Titanic sailing from her final port of call. He had brought along his iPhone's portable charger as he was relying on it not only for photographic memories of the occasion, but film clips to edit for his news segment. He had already taken a sweeping, bird's-eye shot of the harbour from their room.

Dr. Martin was a good looking middle-aged man of medium build and short, dark hair. He was wearing a jaunty tweed paddy cap and had a leather bag over one shoulder. He was chatting with a heavyset American couple who looked like stereotypical tourists, with cameras slung around their necks and fanny packs tied around their waists. There were four other European visitors comprising their jolly band. Martin caught sight of Preston and Todd, realizing his group was now complete and they could begin.

"Welcome to Cobh and the Titanic Trail historical walking tour," he cheerfully said to those assembled, with his gentle Irish accent. "Our walk today takes place on the very Queenstown streets with the same buildings and piers where history was made. You'll get a curbside view of the original shipping company offices including the one the Titanic passengers left from."

The group began to make their way down the street, passing a photographic replica of a 1912 newsboy holding an Evening News Edition proclaiming "Titanic Disaster, Great Loss of Life." The American shutterbugs were already clicking their cameras while Dr. Martin pointed out, "On this very day 113 years earlier, one hundred twenty-three passengers lined up to board tenders to ferry them out to Titanic, which anchored midday at Roches Point in the outer Harbour."

Milton remembered the stop in Queensland but hadn't paid much attention to the picturesque port at the time. What had preoccupied him from looking out over its charming skyline, he asked himself. Had he been too buried in a book, he supposed, to drink in the sights? He regretted not going out on the deck to observe the final cluster of Titanic passengers as they boarded.

The tenders, named Ireland and America, were paddle-wheel steamships of the White Star Line, and its passengers were divided by class with 113 Steerage ticket holders and just 10 first-class passengers.

"For all the lavish luxury associated with the ocean liner, the immigrant trade was the company's bread and butter." Dr. Martin encouraged the group to touch the exact same railings that lined the pathways as they strolled the pier. He explained that the boarding process took approximately ninety minutes, then the last delivery of mail was brought on, and she could set sail.

"The spot had acquired the nickname 'Heartbreak Pier' for the estimated one million Irish emigrants who had bade farewell to loved ones as they departed for new lives in North America."

It was noted that a handful of people disembarked Titanic while it was moored in Cobh, most famously a young priest in training, Francis Brown, whose photographs of life on board the ship as she sailed from Southampton became celebrated over the century that followed.

"He captured the last known images of many passengers and crew," Preston told Todd, thinking of one famous picture of a first-class boy playing with his spinning top that, in hindsight, made the subsequent tragedy even more poignant. It reinforced how much he wanted his video representation of this excursion to communicate a similar personal touch.

Dr. Martin winningly told the yarn of twenty-three-year-old boiler-room crewman John Coffey who wanted to quit his backbreaking service because of a strange foreboding about the ship's fate. He hid under some hessian mail sacks on one of the tenders until the coast was clear and he could jump ship. He would later make headlines for his lucky, life-saving escape.

Fate was a funny thing, Milton acknowledged. Had circumstances turned out differently in St. Moritz with Sebastian, he might never have booked passage on Titanic from Southampton. No regrets for it now, though; without Titanic, he would never have known Jack.

Another notable departure from Cobh was marked by a bronze statue that was their next stop. Seventeen-year-old Irish emigre Annie Moore, the first immigrant to the United States to pass through federal inspection at Ellis Island in 1892. They learned that the artwork, by Irish sculptor Jeanne Rynhart, had a twin on display at her point of arrival in New York.

The preserved or restored architecture was impressive as was the magnificent Cathedral. In addition to the reverent Titanic memorial, there was a breathtakingly powerful one to remember the wreck of the Lusitania, located across from the harbor in Casement Square. It depicted an angel of peace watching over two fishermen who had aided in the rescue of the victims after the sinking. Both sites were adorned with several wreaths of flowers and some candles. They stopped at the former offices of both Cunard and the White Star Line. It did appear as if it had all been frozen in time. A mounted plaque commemorating the Titanic loss explained that "of the 123 who left from Cobh, only 44 survived and completed their journey to New York."

Dr. Martin recounted the testimony of third-class Irishman Eugene Daly, who was traveling with his cousin Maggie, and how other survivors emotionally recalled his skilled, melancholy bagpipe playing as they sailed away from their homeland.

Todd whispered to Preston, "Bagpipe music always makes me sad." He was really getting into it, Preston smiled to himself.

There was another statue, *The Navigator*, that had nothing to do with Titanic but captivated their attention with a dramatic interpretation of an early transatlantic navigator, possibly Saint Brendan.

As expertly as their guide told all of these very intimate anecdotes, Preston was strangely unmoved personally and was instead taking in the experience with the clinical eye of a news producer, filming snippets on his phone as they went along.

There was no connection for Milton either, and Preston felt the need to find something that tied it all to them. After all, what Titanic story could compare with their own?

A little over an hour later, the tour concluded at the local pub, when Dr. Martin invited participants to join him for a beverage and receive a signed "Certificate of Completion" along with his souvenir booklet, *A Heritage Journey Across the Mists of Time*. Preston and Todd hung back until the others obtained their copies and had taken selfies with their host.

Finally getting a private moment with Dr. Martin while the other tourists ordered their cocktails, Preston explained, "I'm planning to create a TV news segment back in New York from all the clips and photos I'm taking."

The charismatic Irishman enthusiastically and generously offered, "How can I help? I'm glad to provide any additional materials you might find useful."

"I'm grateful for that," Preston responded before asking for just that. He had an idea for two final shots to complete and personalize his story and confided his concept to their guide.

Excited by the idea, Dr. Martin cheerily said, "The yard work at home can wait an hour or two. I know just the spots!"

He farewelled the others from his tour to drive
Preston and Todd the short distance uphill to Cannon
O'Leary Place. It was a splendid location unknown to most
tourists, but their guide knew it was exactly where Preston
could get the first shot he was chasing; the last spot on land
where a person would have been able to see Titanic before
she disappeared from sight.

The three of them stood silently for a moment,
looking out over the broad expanse of the historic,
windswept harbour. It was easy to imagine the iconic ship
far in the distance, steaming her way out into the
tempestuous Atlantic. Preston took out his phone and filmed
the scene from that point of view.

Preston said softly to Todd, "Bear with me a little bit
longer, and I swear this will be the last Titanic favor I ever
ask of you."

Innately good-natured and patient, Todd laughed it
off and replied, "Just tell me what you want me to do."

He handed Todd the phone and directed his partner
to record a shot of him, standing alone, looking out at the
water, wistfully. Preston began to slowly wave, knowing
how dramatic it would appear in slow motion.

"Okay, cut!" he directed and stopped waving.

Having already noticed the brisk business of boat rentals in Cobh Harbour, Preston next asked Dr. Martin if he could hire someone to take him out on the water to capture the second shot. A point of view that a Titanic passenger would have had looking back at their final sight of dry land.

"That's an easy one, mate," his helpful host told Preston.

Within twenty minutes, Preston and Todd found themselves accompanied by the proprietor of one of the rental companies, zooming out in a mini speedboat past the old monastic settlement and prison located in the middle of the harbour. The wind picked up, and the air smelled of salt.

"This is it?" Preston asked his captain when he turned off the engine at the far end of the outer harbour.

"Aye. From here, she would have turned out of sight and gotten underway." He pointed back to the piers from where they had departed just minutes before.

Preston took a long sweeping shot from the point of view of a Titanic passenger looking back at dry land for the last time.

"Okay, Steven Spielberg, I need you again," he told Todd.

Again, Todd carefully took the phone and filmed Preston slowly waving back to an imaginary loved one on land.

"And that's a wrap!"

Back on land, they grabbed a couple of sandwiches and cans of soda back in town then sat at an outdoor picnic table, grateful that the threat of rain had never manifested. In fact, the gloomy skies only added, Preston believed, to the moodiness of the piece he would be editing together.

"Are you satisfied with how it all went?" Todd asked him.

"Oh yeah. And thank you again for…well, for *everything*. I don't even know where to begin."

"No thanks necessary. We're a team."

Preston gave him a loving smile. "I feel the same way."

Todd stood up from his seat to reach over and give him a quick peck on the lips. "I'd like to get you back to the room when you finish your lunch."

"Yes, I'm anxious to look at the footage."

"That's not why I want to get you back to the room," he said, more seductively.

Back at the Commodore, before he climbed into bed with Todd, Preston looked out from their windows at the view of the Harbour where they'd had such a productive few hours. Why hadn't it stirred any feelings in him? Where was Milton, whose very final glimpse of God's green earth would have been right there? He was snapped out of his thoughts by the sound of Todd's deep, caring voice.

"Do you want to go up to Belfast for the anniversary festivities? We have flexible tickets."

Without hesitation, Preston answered, "No. We have three whole days before we head home. Let's go have fun in Dublin. I want to kiss the Blarney Stone. Go to nightclubs and fancy restaurants. I told you I wasn't going to ask any more Titanic favors of you. It will always be special, but I think we can all rest in peace now."

Todd patted the mattress to beckon Preston to join him. Outside, the rain finally arrived and poured down on Cobh with a ferocity that matched their lovemaking.

The next morning, they checked out of the hotel and caught a train to Dublin, a journey that took less than three hours. Todd was immersed in making bookings for their stay there while Preston scrolled through the footage from the day before to begin his editing outline for the news segment.

The men's legs were affectionately pressed together while they worked.

As Preston reviewed different clips, he got to the long shot overlooking the harbour from high on Cannon O'Leary Place and began carefully scrutinizing it, imagining how it might look in black and white or even sepia tones to create a vintage look. He was suddenly taken aback by what he saw. He clearly watched Titanic in the moving image, just as he had role-played seeing her from the spot where he was waving.

He blinked to make sure he could believe his eyes. There she was, rounding the outer harbour to make her way out to sea. Three of her four funnels were venting smoke and he could perfectly make out the smokestacks' distinctive "White Star Buff" color, a cross between yellow and orange that was exclusive to their ships.

Preston nudged Todd and said, "Look at this."

Todd examined it and casually remarked, "Beautiful shot."

Todd didn't see Titanic. Before Preston could dispute or try to describe what he'd seen, he looked back at his phone and now the ghost ship was gone. His pulse quickened. A wishful, wistful figment he had perhaps conjured, after all.

Quickly and deftly scrolling through the video files with his index finger, he wanted to examine the shot of him waving out to sea. It appeared just as he thought it would, so he wanted to check the subsequent matching shot of him waving back from the rented boat they'd sailed out into the harbour.

There was the shot, but it wasn't Preston. It was Milton. He didn't look doleful or plaintive in the least. In fact, he was smiling as he waved farewell.

Epilogue

Wednesday, April 17, 1912

She had been scheduled to arrive at New York City's Pier 54 at five in the evening, but it looked as though Captain Smith would be able to beat that projection by nearly three hours, in spite of having slowed to a crawl three nights earlier to safely navigate through the ice fields less than 400 miles southeast of Newfoundland. Her successful maiden voyage would be front-page news throughout Western civilization, but the trip itself was largely uneventful, other than the extinguishing of a coal fire in stokehold 9 and the madcap misadventure of John Jacob Astor's prized Airedale, Kitty, who escaped the kennel and led stewards and waitresses on a chase that eventually led all the way to the Grand Staircase where none other than Margaret Brown was able to corral her to be leashed.

The icy air from earlier in the sailing had turned to a comparatively mild temperature in the low 50s. The skies were overcast, but no rain had yet fallen.

J. Bruce Ismay, the White Star Line's effete managing director, considered Titanic's arrival in New York Harbor nothing less than a triumph for his company as well as a testament to her builders, Harland & Wolff, and her designer, Thomas Andrews. The men were strolling the First-Class public spaces, all smiles, shaking hands, and beginning the farewell rituals that went along with the final hours of a transatlantic crossing. Ismay was hoping to steal a private moment with the charming Marian Thayer before disembarkation—by far his favorite acquaintance on this crossing, even though she seemed inevitably surrounded by her admiring circle of family and friends.

It was a happy and excitable atmosphere as everyone on board waited for their first glance of the Statue of Liberty to welcome them to the United States. That included everyone from experienced, world-weary globetrotters like Colonel Gracie and the Countess of Rothes, all the way down to the most inexperienced first-time travelers in steerage, clamoring to see the sights from their spots on the Aft Well and Poop Decks.

Perhaps no one was smiling more widely than Milton Long, who had finished a late breakfast at his new table, which included the Thayer family and traveling mates, Archibald Butt and Francis Millet. If his former mealtime companions, Gretchen Longley and her aunts, were miffed by his defection to the other side of the dining room, he didn't much care. Since he and Jack Thayer had struck up their friendship on the night of the 14th, they had become inseparable. He wouldn't have minded if the trip had lasted indefinitely.

It was not uncommon on trips like these for zealous, new friendships to be quickly forged, and this one had been no different. Their peers on board were now as used to seeing Milton and Jack together as they were to seeing Lady Duff-Gordon and Madeleine Astor with their heads together gossiping, or tennis players Richard Norris Williams and Karl Behr joshing with other gentlemen in the smoking room and gymnasium. In fact, the latter pair were busily collecting payments on bets they'd made with fellow passengers as to Titanic's exact arrival time. Meanwhile, Adolphe Saalfeld had talked Dorothy Gibson's mother into allowing the young film star to be the first to try out his exclusive new fragrance line in order to secure her official public endorsement.

Chief Purser McElroy, always known for his sense of humor, was all business this morning, making sure his staff was hastily preparing for the upcoming disembarkation. He walked by the Thayer table and paused to say, "In the event that I don't get to see you again until your next excursion, may I please extend all of our heartfelt thanks and appreciation for your company. It's been a pleasure and a privilege."

Marian Thayer extended her gloved hand for him to perfunctorily kiss and told him, "We have loved every moment, Mr. McElroy. We are grateful."

"Indeed we are, sir," echoed her husband, John. "We will be sailing with you again."

"How long will you be docked in New York?" Millet asked.

"Three days and then back to Southampton. We look forward to serving you all again."

Bruce Ismay was hovering nearby, trying not to appear as if he were lurking, still waiting to capture a moment of Marian's attention while he still had the opportunity.

As McElroy made his way on to the next table, John Thayer turned to Milton, who seemed to be having a laugh with Jack over some private joke between them.

"Mr. Long, I do wish you'd consider taking us up on our invitation to Haverford. I'm going to be having quite a birthday celebration, and we believe that the more, the merrier."

Respectfully, Milton replied, "I can't tell you how appreciative I am for the offer, Mr. Thayer, and I hope you will allow me to take a raincheck. Birthdays are special and deserve to be celebrated."

He could feel Jack's knee press against his underneath the table and hidden by the white linen tablecloth.

"Of course. We love to entertain. And our cricket club is right next door. Do you play?"

"I prefer winter sports, sir," Milton answered with one of his signature smirks that so charmed Jack. "But believe it or not, unlike many people, I actually enjoy watching cricket matches."

The others laughed at his little joke, especially in light of how shy and reserved the New Englander had seemed socially.

"Blame it on me, Dad," Jack said, pink faced with exuberance. "Before Milton heads back to Massachusetts, I've talked him into spending a few days seeing New York City with me. It will be ripping. You keep saying you plan on keeping your fiftieth festivities going for a full year, so I know you won't miss me, either."

Marian had difficulty being stern, especially with her children, but did her best to at least sound authoritative when she said, "Three days will suffice, son. We will expect you on Sunday."

As Milton's knee pressed back against his, Jack answered with mock obeisance, "Yes, Mother dear."

"That's more than enough time for you to do some sightseeing. As long as you promise me that will include the Historical Society and a legitimate Broadway show. I've heard marvelous things about *A Butterfly on the Wheel*."

Archibald Butt piped up, "No showgirls or gambling halls, chaps. I can arrange admission for you both to the Union League Club."

His companion Francis Millet poo-poo'ed him with, "Archie, they're young men. Leave them to Coney Island and Times Square. Alas, it's too early for baseball. But there's no shortage of entertainment in Manhattan, that is certain."

"I'm sure we'll find plenty of activities to keep us entertained," Milton assured the pair, contemplating the prospect of becoming similarly lifelong partners with Jack.

"No doubt," Millet commented, inadvertently cocking an eyebrow.

The waiters and busboys were clearing away the settings from nearby tables in a not-so subtle indication that the dining party should be moving on.

"I'd best go check on Margaret," Marian said, referring to her maid who would be finishing up their packing.

"Let's all meet on the Promenade to watch the city skyline," her husband suggested to his party.

As Jack stood to hold his mother's chair as she rose from her seat, Milton excused himself saying, "I need to return to my cabin and finish getting my things in order. I will be outside in two shakes of a lamb's tail." He'd already adopted Jack's knack for using slang.

"My kit's all together. Let me come give you a hand, mate," Jack offered in a disguised signal to Milton.

Without turning back to his parents as he and Milton walked away from the table, he called back, "See you soon, Mother and Dad."

Butt and Millet looked at each other with a knowing glance. It was obvious to them that there was something between young Jack and Milton.

Once they arrived at Milton's cabin, they found the deck's no-nonsense steward, William, placing Milton's overcoat and straw hat on the hangers beside the armoire. His two Louis Vuitton suitcases were readied, but his leather Gladstone bag was still open on the luggage rack, awaiting Milton to pack up the last of his toiletries.

"We'll be back shortly to collect your luggage, Mr. Long," William told him, nodding to the gentlemen before exiting the cabin.

"Say, I have an idea," Jack proposed, once the crewman was gone. "Let's find a New York haberdasher and get ourselves matching suits. Our secret."

"What other secrets shall we have?" Milton asked softly before wrapping his arms around Jack's slender, firm body.

They had been aching to touch all morning and immediately gave in to a passionate, open-mouthed kiss that intensified so quickly that Jack had to place his hand on the sides of Milton's face to hold them both steady.

"I can't believe we're doing this."

"Believe it," Jack told him, smiling widely. "We're a team."

Where had he heard that before? It didn't matter now. Nothing else mattered but Jack. He moved his lips to Jack's, who was still smiling so broadly that Milton could feel his teeth for a brief moment before Jack worked his tongue back for a vigorous, carnal kiss.

In spite of, or perhaps because of, the taboo nature of their clinch, they became instantly heated and rubbed against one another with fervor. They would have collapsed onto the bed and taken it further had they not been able to hear all the commotion from the corridor as people bustled about to prepare for arrival.

"Are we all set for accommodations?" inquired Milton breathlessly, after breaking their lip lock. They continued to hold each other tightly while curbing their lustful desires.

"I confirmed with the wireless operator this morning that my message went through to the Plaza. I've secured us a room overlooking Central Park for four nights. I thought the Waldorf would run too much risk of us running into people we know."

"Splendid. I wish it were for four weeks. Or months!"

"I'm relieved my parents were so agreeable about it all. I'm sure they'll expect me to pay a call to their friends at the Consul General's office, but that won't take long."

Milton noticed his two books were still on the nightstand by the bed, and he reluctantly released his hold on Jack to stuff them into the suitcase along with his shaving kit, comb, and half-dozen matchbooks he'd collected. It amused him to think about how he'd given up entirely on reading once he'd met Jack and been completely sidetracked by their infatuation.

"We'll go meet them out on the Promenade," he said, moving quickly, "but as much as I like your mother and father, as soon as we pass through customs and retrieve our bags, we are getting immediately into a cab."

"No argument from me, Chuckaboo," Jack said, reaching out to brush his hand against Milton's arm, affectionately.

A wave of excited reactions were suddenly audible from the other side of the door after someone had announced, "We're pulling into New York Harbor!"

Jack had the sudden vivacity of a schoolboy and instinctively loosened his tie, urging Milton to hurry up so they could watch as Titanic made her way to the pier, decked out in her flags as she proudly steamed into the mighty Hudson River.

The young men joined John and Marian Thayer to watch as they glided past the Statue of Liberty and proceeded smoothly to Pier 59, where hundreds of cheering spectators had gathered to welcome Titanic at the completion of her triumphant maiden voyage. Ferries, tugboats, and other vessels all blew their horns and whistles in celebration of the unsinkable Queen of the Seas' arrival.

It seemed as if every passenger aboard had clamored outside to take in the sight of the White Star Line dock coming into view, seemingly framed by an endless stretch of so-called "skyscrapers." Bandleader Wallace Hartley and his musicians were on deck playing some gay ragtime tunes appropriate for the high spirits of the moment. The skies may have been drab, but the mood was as bright as a midsummer afternoon.

Once docked, first- and second-class passengers would pass relatively quickly through customs, while third-class men and women would be ferried to Ellis Island for medical and legal inspection. Before Milton and Jack separated from them, the Thayer patriarch reminded Milton to visit them in Philadelphia.

To everyone's surprise, Milton informed them that he was considering giving university life another go and wanted to investigate what opportunities there might be for him in the "City of Brotherly Love" to pursue studies in medicine.

"Jefferson Medical College has a sterling reputation, I'm told."

With hearty enthusiasm, John told him, "It's one of the finest in the country. We can always use more good doctors." Milton promised he would look into it and received a collegial pat on the back from Jack's father, along with an offer to make any subsequent introductions that might prove helpful.

When Milton and Jack were finally alone together in the back of an electric hansom cab en route to the Plaza, their legs pressed discreetly together, Jack asked, "I had no idea you were interested in the field of medicine."

"I hadn't really, either," Milton chuckled. "It's only just come to me in the last few days. I can't keep sailing and wandering around the world forever." Teasingly, he added, "And Philadelphia sounds like a wonderful place to reinvent myself."

It was early evening before they managed to arrive in their simple but elegant hotel suite on the Plaza's sixth floor, the view from the windows looking as if they were perched atop some of the barely blossoming trees in Central Park. They could see the lake, which attracted many New Yorkers during the winter months for ice skating.

As the bellhop organized their luggage opposite the two full-sized beds that dominated the room, Milton mused, "All I did in St. Moritz was ski. You'll have to teach me how to figure skate one day."

"How did you know I skate?"

Milton's smirk was genuine and his eyes twinkled more blue than grey today. "You mentioned it the night we met. Walking on deck."

"I did? I don't recall."

"I remember everything."

As soon as they were finally alone, they removed their heavy suit jackets and unlaced their shoes to remove. This was the moment they had been agonizing days for—an opportunity to be together without fear of discovery or impropriety. It was at once both thrilling and terrifying.

With every item of clothing they removed, their hands exploring the magical discoveries that lay beneath the garments, pulses quickened. The excitement mounted not only because of how forbidden this passion was perceived as being, but by how fervently they desired it and how impatiently they had awaited it. The men made love with an almost urgent intensity, soaking the sheets with perspiration in spite of the cool spring temperature in the room.

It was as if they were frantically dancing some crazy horizontal tango, and after three consecutive rounds, they collapsed in each other's embrace, twisted in a tangle of bedding and calmed into a quieter, more tender state.

"Wowza," Jack finally said, prompting Milton to laugh and reply, "Wowza, indeed."

"It's astounding to believe this all happened in less than a week." Jack commented as he nuzzled against his partner.

"I'd never want to deprive you of anything. A wife, a family."

"I'm a little young to be thinking about that now. I can't think of anywhere else I'd rather be than right here with you. Besides, how could I possibly feel deprived when we are together this way?"

"Meeting you has somehow enabled me to glimpse the future. To want a future."

"You give me too much credit, Milton."

As a chilly spring shower suddenly began to pour down outside, the couple kissed softly, and both could feel the stirring in their loins return yet again. Milton paused before allowing his libido to yield and focused his gray-blue eyes on Jack's rosy countenance with some seriousness.

"I give you *all* the credit."

Author's Note

As documented in my previous books and in Alexandra Boyd's 2023 documentary, *Ship of Dreams: Titanic Movie Diaries*, I have had a lifelong connection to Milton Clyde Long who perished in the Titanic tragedy. His biography is largely unknown, so any attempt to dramatize it would rely on imagination, and I've spent decades imagining the "what ifs" about his life.

Just as we watched the repressive world in which Kate Winslet's character in James Cameron's 1997 film *Titanic* (and most women of the Edwardian Age) lived, I often thought how difficult it must have been for homosexual men of the time. While I have no evidence to suggest that Milton was gay, I saw in his sad, premature demise a representation of lost opportunity. What blessings might life have had in store for someone like him, with so much privilege and opportunity? It was all over for him before his 30th birthday, and our seemingly supernatural connection to each other made me wonder if I hadn't somehow been cosmically handed the baton to finish the race on his behalf.

My original concept for this book was to tell my own "relationship" with Milton, but I had just finished two semi-autobiographical novels that spanned the years between 1980 and 2012. Rather than go back again to the era of padded shoulders, big hair, and parachute pants, I opted to fictionalize the story and set it in the present day. Whether you picked up the book because you're a Titanic enthusiast, an LGBTQ+ advocate, or have an interest in the paranormal, I hope you found this tale entertaining and even enlightening.

It was written with the utmost respect for the victims of the Titanic, including those who survived the sinking before facing "survivor's guilt" and post-traumatic stress for the rest of their lives. It was also written with great affection for the Titanic community I have gotten to know through co-hosting the "Titanic Talk" podcast. It is an ever-expanding extended family.

If there is any silver lining to the awful loss from that "Night to Remember" in 1912, it is that it resulted not only in safer conditions for passengers traveling at sea, but spawned generations of enthusiastic historians, artists, scientists, writers, and explorers who keep retelling the timeless story of RMS Titanic, "The Ship of Dreams."

Nelson Aspen

Acknowledgments

A big thank you to the team at Red Sky Entertainment, especially Myron Hyman and Matt Machin. Hearty thanks to my editor, Jason Conover, who helped me navigate the fantasy genre while learning how to bridge the generation gap. To Alexandra Boyd, Paul Carganilla, Sydney Salomon, Lesley-Anne (L.A.) Beadles, cover artist Greg DiNapoli and the ever-growing family of "Titanic Talk" fans who reignited my personal passion for the Ship of Dreams. To my late parents, for their love of history and nurturing my own belief that "the past is prologue." And, as ever, to my husband Jonny for his patience and humor while I go through the writing process.

Made in the USA
Columbia, SC
09 March 2025